Liba's Palace

Miriam Walfish

For Ari, with love and thanks

The author would like to acknowledge the invaluable assistance of Naomi Musiker, Archivist of the South African Jewish Board of Deputies, as well as Hilda Boshoff and Sandra Smit of the CP Nel Museum, Oudtshoorn

Jewish Girls Around the World —
The Liba Miller Series
Book 1: Liba's Palace

ISBN: 978-1-60763-083-8

Editor: Nina Ackerman Indig
Proofreader: Hadassa Goldsmith
Illustrations: DreaMaker Studio
Cover & internal design: Justine Elliott

THE JUDAICA PRESS, INC.
123 Ditmas Avenue / Brooklyn, NY 11218
718-972-6200 / 800-972-6201
info@judaicapress.com
www.judaicapress.com

Manufactured in the United States of America

Chapter One

Liba felt a familiar, quick tug on her braid. She looked down and saw her youngest brother, Chaim, standing beside her. "Liba, I want to see. Pick me up!" he begged, his big brown eyes wide with excitement.

Liba scooped five-year-old Chaim into her arms. She pointed to the huge dark shape in the distance. "Isn't it beautiful?" she asked.

Chaim nodded enthusiastically, the peak of his small cloth cap falling over his forehead. "Quick! Put me down!"

"Put you down? Why? I just picked you up."

"I want to tell Peretz and Hershel to come take a look. And Mama and Tatty, too. Wait here. I'm going downstairs and then I'll be right back." Chaim freed himself from his sister's arms.

Liba reached down and gently adjusted her brother's cap. "You won't get too far if you can't see," she said. The little boy laughed and then hurried away in search of the rest of the Miller family.

Liba leaned against the ship's rail and looked out again at the sunlit sea. She had been standing there for hours, ever since early morning when the captain had announced they would be docking that day. With growing excitement she had watched as the ship drew closer and closer to the bay and the faint outline of the mountain grew clearer and clearer. Liba now slowly became aware of the sounds of other people beginning to gather nearby. Like the Millers, they had boarded the ship nineteen days ago, at the port in Southampton, England. Most of them had also traveled in steerage class — the crowded, poorly lit area of the ship that was far below deck. They, too, were eager to reach dry land.

Chaim soon reappeared. He ran toward Liba, calling, "Did I miss it? Is it gone?"

Liba smiled. *Miss the mountain?* Impossible. It rose thousands of feet high in the sky, and could be seen for miles. Liba understood Chaim's mistake — he had never seen a mountain before. The family was from Kelm, a small town in Lithuania (part of the Russian empire), where the land was mostly flat with only a few occasional hills.

"No, you didn't miss the mountain. It is even closer now." Picking him up a second time, Liba continued, "Look. Do you see that? Instead of it coming to a peak, a sharp point, like most mountains, it is flat, just like a table. That is where it gets its name."

"A table! Oh, yes, this is a good name for this type of mountain," nodded Chaim, as if he had grown up surrounded by mountains.

Itzig Miller, the children's father, now appeared with nine-year-old Peretz and eight-year-old Hershel. Sorel Miller, their mother, followed closely behind, stopping here and there to greet a number of the other Jewish women on board.

As an increasing number of people gathered near the side of the ship, Chaim called to his parents. "Come! Come and look! It looks like a giant table." Pointing out to sea with a chubby finger, he added, "See? It's called Table Mountain because of its shape."

The family joined Liba near the ship's rail.

Together they stood and admired the giant mass of rock that loomed in front of them. Set against the backdrop of the brilliant blue sky, Table Mountain was breathtaking, majestic. Its enormous top was wide and square; Liba thought it looked as if it had been sliced straight across with a knife. It was framed on either side by two smaller peaks; one of the other passengers had told the Miller family these peaks were named the Lion's Head and the Devil's Peak.

"Ah! What a beautiful sight," said Itzig, a look of delight spreading across his face. Turning to his wife, he asked, "Sorel, it is something special, no?"

"Yes, Itzig, it is," she replied. "Exactly the way Uncle Binam described it, all those years ago."

Itzig pointed to a small object in the distance.

"Look over there. Do you see that?" he asked his family.

"What is it?" asked Peretz.

"I believe it is a seagull. It is a type of bird."

"I've never heard of that sort of bird before," said Hershel. "Does it do something special?"

"Yes, it does. It tells us that we are getting

"What a beautiful sight," Liba's father says.

close, very close, to the harbor. Seagulls don't fly far from land. If we are able to see one nearby, it means we will dock soon."

Turning to face everyone in his family, Itzig continued, "Let's go back downstairs. We must find our baggage. We have to prepare ourselves to leave the ship. We are almost there!"

"I want to carry the samovar this time," declared Chaim.

"You're not strong enough," argued Peretz.

"Yes, I am!" insisted Chaim. "Look at my muscles." He quickly began to roll up the sleeve of his jacket.

Peretz looked at Hershel; both older boys looked at their little brother and laughed.

"All right, if you're really that strong, you can help," said Peretz.

Itzig began to lead his family away from the ship's rail. Only eleven-year-old Liba remained, intent on watching the ship reach the harbor. If she squinted, she could see the outline of a familiar shape. *Yes, those are buildings, light-colored buildings*, she thought. *How unusual; they look like they're made of sand.*

"We are almost there," Liba said out loud,

repeating her tatty's words. "We are almost there!" she said a second time, even louder. It was too wonderful to believe. After all these weeks and months, after all the planning, the preparation and the endless traveling, the Millers would soon set foot on dry land — here, in Cape Town, the Union of South Africa.

Chapter Two

The passengers walked down the long wooden gangplank, away from the ship and toward the dock. There were single men traveling alone, married women tightly gripping the hands of their children, and young couples, many holding babies in their arms. All were exhausted by the long journey, but glad to have finally reached their destination. They carried worn trunks and battered suitcases, and baskets and bundles of all shapes and sizes. Some wore caps and suits; others, loose-fitting dresses and kerchiefs. Some only spoke Yiddish; others spoke English or German; a few knew Russian and a little bit of Lithuanian. No matter how different they were, all of them shared the same hope — that here, thousands of miles away from where they had been born, they would build better lives for themselves.

"Stay together, stay together," Sorel instructed her children yet again.

"Don't worry, Mama, we are wearing our new jackets," Hershel said.

In preparation for the trip, Sorel had sewn matching dark gray jackets for each of her three sons. In this way, she reasoned, if one of the boys got lost ("*chas v'shalom*!" she had quickly added), it would be easy for people to tell whom he belonged to. Tatty had not thought this was necessary. After all, he had said, it was clear as day that they were brothers. They all looked like him. Unlike Liba, who had inherited their mama's fair skin and blue eyes, the boys had darker skin, thick brown hair and big dark eyes. Sorel had insisted, though, and the boys had worn their jackets for most of the journey.

"Stay together, stay together!" Sorel repeated, as if she hadn't heard what Hershel had just said.

When the family reached the base of the gangplank, two men in olive-colored uniforms directed them to a nearby line that had begun to form outside a small wooden building.

Liba noticed that her tatty looked uneasy, and she understood why. He did not know English, and he would soon have to speak to the authorities in order for the family to be allowed into the country. She remembered that before they had boarded the boat at the Russian port city of Libau, the officials had asked him all sorts of questions. Her tatty spoke a little bit of Russian and he had managed to make himself understood. Then, when they arrived in England, everyone in the family had had to undergo a medical examination. They had been very lucky. A fellow passenger spoke English and he had helped translate everything that was said into Yiddish.

The line moved forward. Soon it was the Millers' turn. "Remember," said Itzig to his children, his tone serious, "no one is to say a word. Everyone is to wait patiently and quietly."

"Yes, Tatty," all four children answered.

Careful not to forget any of their belongings, they went inside the building. A heavyset man with thick glasses was seated behind a long wooden desk. He wore the same type of uniform as the men at the dock.

"Documents," he said.

Itzig Miller assumed this meant that the man wanted to see their travel papers. Over the past few weeks, Itzig had carefully guarded these in the pocket of his long dark overcoat. He took them out, stepped forward and placed them on the desk.

The man picked up the papers and quickly thumbed through them. Liba thought he looked bored, or tired.

"Where are you going?"

Itzig wasn't entirely certain what the man was asking, but he guessed that he wanted to know where they were planning to live.

"Oat ... oat ... Oudtshoorn," he replied, struggling to pronounce the difficult, unfamiliar word.

If only the man spoke Yiddish, Liba thought. *Then Tatty could explain the whole story to him, all about Uncle Binam and the will and the hotel ...*

"Town of Oudtshoorn, is it? Hoping to become an ostrich farmer, are you?" The man chuckled to himself.

Itzig did not know how to respond. He simply nodded.

"Everything appears to be in order. When I fill out this form, you will be free to leave."

Leave? Leave? Wasn't this the English word for

If only the man spoke Yiddish, Liba thinks.

"iberlozen"? Liba's heart began to beat loudly. *Was Tatty being told they had to leave the country? Why?*

Itzig shifted his weight from one foot to the other. The man picked up a quill and began to write on a sheet of paper. Although she knew it was silly, Liba thought that if she studied the man carefully, she might understand what he was writing. But then she noticed something odd. He was writing backwards, moving the quill across the paper from left to right, instead of right to left. Then she remembered — he was writing in English, not in Yiddish or Hebrew!

Peretz, Hershel and Chaim were growing increasingly restless. They started to fidget and look around the room. A large photograph of Queen Victoria that hung on the wall behind the official's desk soon caught Peretz's eye.

"Hershel, look over there," he said quietly. "Do you see that?"

"Sure, I do."

"The woman looks so familiar. I feel that I know her, somehow," said Peretz.

Hershel took a careful look at the photograph.

"I see what you mean. She does look very familiar."

Chaim, who had been listening to his brothers' conversation, piped up, "I know who she is. It's Tante Freyda. I recognize those eyes."

"Here? In Cape Town? Why would Tante Freyda's photograph be on the wall in an office in Cape Town?" asked Peretz.

"Maybe she came here once for a visit and she left it behind, as a gift?" suggested Chaim.

"No, don't be silly. Tante Freyda was never in Cape Town. And even if she had been, she'd have left a plate of *teiglach* behind, not a photograph. She always used to bring *teiglach* when she came to visit us, remember?"

"If it isn't Tante Freyda, who is it?" asked Chaim.

"Let's ask Liba. She'll know," said Hershel. He leaned closer to his sister and asked, "Who is that woman?"

"What woman?" asked Liba, startled by the question.

"Over there, on the wall. We think she looks familiar, but we can't seem to figure out who she is."

Liba tore her eyes away from the official and looked up. "Oh, that's Queen Victoria. She was the queen of the British Empire for many years. The Union of South Africa is part of the British Empire, which means that she was the queen here, too. She looks familiar because there was a photograph of her just like this one hanging on the wall in that building, the Poor Jews' Temporary Shelter, where we stayed for a few nights when we first arrived in England."

Turning to Chaim, Peretz said, "Did you hear that? It's a photograph of a queen, not of Tante Freyda."

"Really?" asked Chaim. He continued to stare at the photograph, unconvinced. *The woman really looked very much like Tante Freyda. Those eyes ... that nose ... the expression on the face ...*

The man put down his quill and handed the family's documents back to Itzig.

"Be careful with those ostriches, Miller. They can be nasty if you make them angry," he said.

Itzig stared at the man and remained standing in his place.

"Next," called the official.

Another man, a fellow Jewish passenger,

entered the room, followed by his wife and two young children.

Itzig now understood that he and his family were allowed to leave the building. Using a few of the only words he knew in English, he said, "Thank you, sir."

Turning to his family, he said in Yiddish, "Everything is in order. Follow me."

The Miller family grabbed their belongings, quickly left the building and stepped outside into the bright afternoon sun.

Chapter Three

"That's the strangest-looking tree I have ever seen. It doesn't have any leaves, just a thick, funny-looking trunk," said Peretz, pointing across the street.

"You have to look up high. The leaves are gathered way at the top. I think it's a *tamar*, a palm tree," Liba explained. "A long time ago, Uncle Binam sent us a postcard with a photograph of one. He said that this is the type of tree from which *lulavim* come."

Using his right hand, Peretz shielded his eyes from the sun and looked skyward. "How can such a special tree grow here in Cape Town? How is that possible?" he asked his sister.

"Anything is possible here," Liba answered happily, a bright smile on her face.

The Miller family had been in South Africa for only a few short hours, but Liba was already convinced that it was one of the most exciting places in the entire

world. There were so many things to see: red-roofed houses lined up in rows, their front gardens overflowing with thick green vines and many-colored flowers; British flags hanging from the balconies of tall stone buildings; huge clock towers proudly indicating the time of day, and powerful horses pulling two-wheeled carts — cape carts, they were called — through the busy streets. And the people! Never before had Liba seen such people! Some had light skin, with hair so straight and yellow it reminded Liba of straw, while others had skin so dark it was nearly black, with hair so thick and coarse it almost looked like wool.

All of a sudden, Chaim started jumping up and down. "Oh! Oh! Look! It's a … it's a … "

Chaim did not know what to say next. How could he describe the huge, shiny black box with four large wheels that moved along the street without a driver?

"Tatty! Tatty! What is that?" the boy's eyes were enormous, filled with a mixture of fascination and fear.

"Remarkable! It is a motorcar. I have read about such things," replied Itzig, his eyes also

There are so many exciting things to see in Cape Town, thinks Liba.

growing wide with interest. "I believe the first one arrived here just a few years ago."

The rest of the family stood and watched in wonder as the car made its noisy approach along the street.

Someone suddenly tapped Itzig on the shoulder. Itzig turned around and found himself looking at a man with dark wavy hair and round glasses. "*Shalom aleichem,*" said the man, extending his right hand.

"*Aleichem shalom,*" Itzig replied, extending his own hand.

Surely this man must have mistaken Tatty for someone else, Liba thought. *We don't know anyone here in South Africa.*

The man continued in Yiddish. "Welcome to Cape Town. My name is Bension Hersch.* You must be tired. Follow me, I will show you how to get to District Six. It's not far at all. Many, many Jews have settled there."

"Thank you very much for your offer, but I am afraid we are not staying in the city. We are on

---

* Bension Hersch was a well-known Jewish figure at the docks in the early 1900s who greeted Jewish immigrants upon their arrival in Cape Town.

our way to Oudtshoorn. I understand that we need to take a train," replied Itzig.

The man looked surprised. "Oh … ostrich dealer, are you?"

There is that word again, thought Liba. Ostrich. She opened her mouth wide and tried to say it: "Os … os … ostrichchh …" It seemed that every time someone heard their family was going to Oudtshoorn, they mentioned this word. Sorel had explained to Liba that an ostrich was some sort of big bird, but that she had never seen such a thing in Kelm.

"No, not an ostrich dealer. My uncle — that is, my late uncle, *zichrono livracha* — lived there for many years, and he left me — that is, in his will, he left me — his hotel."

"A hotel? In Oudtshoorn? What luck! Oudtshoorn is a lovely community. It is often called "the Jerusalem of Africa," and sometimes "Little Jerusalem." About 300 Jewish families live there and there are two shuls."

"Yes, I know. My uncle wrote me about it, many times," Itzig said with a nod.

"It's a long journey. You will need food for the train." Motioning to a large wicker basket on the ground, Mr. Hersch said, "You must take this with you."

"What is it?" asked Itzig, puzzled.

"It is for you and your family." The man bent down and opened the lid. The family looked on as he showed them eggs, black bread and something wrapped in a pale cloth.

"That's fried fish. And there is tea in the flasks, at the bottom," he explained.

"But ... but ... we can't take this from you," Itzig objected.

"Of course you can. You must understand, Mr. Miller. This is what we Jews do, here in the Union of South Africa. We are a community of immigrants. Some of us have been here for thirty years, and others, like you, have just arrived. We help each other. We look out for each other. We always have. With Hashem's help, we always will."

What an incredible act of chessed, Liba thought. *A complete stranger meets us at the port and gives us an entire basket of kosher food. What a wonderful place this is, South Africa.*

Carefully closing the lid on the basket, Mr. Hersch continued. "Now, please, let me direct you to the railway station."

A short time later, the Miller family boarded an eastbound train headed for the Klein Karoo, the region where Oudtshoorn was located. Chaim, as always, settled himself into Liba's lap and fell asleep within minutes. Hershel took out a tiny checkerboard from his jacket pocket; Peretz took out the pieces. They began to play but their eyes soon grew heavy. Lulled by the constant motion of the train, they also fell asleep — Hershel still holding a red checker in his hands. Itzig and Sorel sat facing each other, the basket of food stored safely between them. They talked quietly for a short while, but then they, too, nodded off.

Liba pressed her face against the train's narrow window. She was determined to stay awake. She did not want to miss a single second of their new life in South Africa.

Chapter Four

Liba looked at the orchards in the distance. The trees were covered with thousands of fresh, bright green leaves, and she imagined all kinds of ripe fruit — dark red plums, shiny yellow pears and orange peaches — hanging on the branches, waiting to be picked. *How strange,* she thought. *Back home in Kelm, most of the trees are now bare, their leaves having turned brown and fallen to the ground weeks earlier. And it's cold there now, too,* she realized. *Maybe it has even snowed.* Liba suddenly remembered what her mama had explained, all those months ago. South Africa was at the very southern tip of the continent of Africa, on "the other side of the world." The seasons fell in the reverse order; when it was winter in Kelm, it was summer in South Africa. When it was fall in South Africa, it was spring in Kelm. "Does that mean the Jews in South Africa have *Pesach* in the fall?" Hershel had asked. Mama had thought about this for a minute and then said yes, she believed this was the way it must be.

The train continued to climb higher and higher up the slope of the mountain. The valleys below were dotted with dark green forests and clear blue rivers. Enormous mountains soared high in the distance, their peaks covered in bright white snow. Everything was so colorful, so vivid; Liba felt as if she were looking at a painting, not at an actual landscape. *Everything is so different here,* she thought.

As the train continued its climb, Liba thought back to last summer, when everything had changed ....

It was a *motzei Shabbos* in the middle of July. Liba was studying *Pirkei Avos* together with Bayla Goldberg, her best friend and next-door neighbor. When it was Liba's turn she had read, "*Eizehu ashir? Hasamei'ach b'chelko.* Who is wealthy? One who is happy with what he has." Bayla had commented, "I don't know ... I guess ... I guess I'm happy with what I have ... but somehow I always thought I would be happier if I had more." Liba had smiled

Everything is so different here, thinks Liba.

understandingly and nodded in agreement.

As soon as Shabbos was over, her parents had gone out. This was very unusual. Her tatty only left the house in the evenings to *daven* Minchah and Maariv at the *shtiebel* down the street. His nights were spent with his sons, reviewing what they had learned that day in *cheder*. Later, when the boys had gone to sleep, he would sit by himself and study a *blatt Gemara*, a glass of sweet tea nearby. Her mama was always home at night, too, mending clothing or darning socks by the light of a small oil lamp.

The boys had asked their parents why they were still wearing their Shabbos clothes, but neither of them had answered. Right before she had left the house, Mama had told Liba they were going to talk to one of their neighbors, "Mordke *di Amerikaner* (Mordechai the American)" — so called because once, many years ago, he had spent some time in a town in America called Cleveland, and he knew a bit of English.

While their parents were out, Liba had tried to keep her brothers busy by playing jackstones with them. Hershel soon grew bored. As he walked around the small wooden house looking for something interesting to do, he accidentally knocked over Mama's big burlap bag of goose feathers. He bent down and picked it up; a few feathers flew out and tickled his nose. He sneezed with such force that he dropped the bag on the floor. Countless tiny feathers escaped and flew into the air. Chaim ran to help but he lost his balance and fell. As he lay on the floor, he cried, "Help, help, I've slipped in the snow!" Peretz and Hershel started to laugh, and soon, all three boys began to dance around the room, tossing goose feathers into the air and chanting, "It's snowing, it's snowing."

Just as Liba headed to the kitchen to look for a broom, her parents walked through the front door. Liba thought they somehow looked both shocked and confused at the same time. She didn't know if this was because of the mess her brothers had made, or if it had to do with her parents' visit to Mordke *di Amerikaner.*

Once the floor had been swept, the feathers stuffed back into the bag, and the boys tucked into bed, her parents told her that they wanted to speak with her.

Her tatty explained that a package containing

an official-looking letter and an important-looking document had arrived yesterday, right before Shabbos. He knew it was from the Union of South Africa; he recognized the stamps. In 1869, diamonds had been discovered in the northern part of the Cape, in an area called Kimberley. A number of Jews, many from Kelm and the neighboring town of Shavli, soon set out for South Africa. It was a young, developing country and many believed it offered endless opportunities for those who were willing to work hard. Binam Miller, Itzig's father's younger brother, was one of those hopeful emigrants. Though he never did find any diamonds, Binam remained in South Africa for the rest of his life. Sadly, he had died a few months ago, never having married.

Her tatty then took a big breath, as if preparing to say something equally big.

"According to Mordke *di Amerikaner*, the letter is from a law firm in Cape Town. If he has translated it correctly, it seems that Uncle Binam has left me a property in South Africa."

"Left you a property? What does that mean?" Liba asked.

"Many years ago, Uncle Binam wrote a will. The document that came with the letter was a copy of this will. According to Mordke *di Amerikaner,* Uncle Binam stated that I was to inherit his hotel upon his death, that he was leaving it to me as a gift. Who ever knew he owned a hotel?"

"He owned a hotel? You mean, an actual hotel belonged to *him*?" Liba's voice rose in amazement. She had never heard of a Jew owning such a large property here in the Pale.*

"Yes, it seems it is called 'Miller's Hotel.'"

"What are you supposed to do with this hotel?" Liba asked.

"Why, run it, of course. There is one condition, though. I must allow the people who work in the hotel to remain there for as long as they wish. Of course, this makes perfect sense. After all, I work in a lumber yard — what do I possibly know about running a hotel?"

"Run it? Tatty, how will you be able to run it? We live so very far away."

---

* The Pale of Settlement, which included Lithuania, was established in 1791 and was abolished in 1917. It was the only part of the Russian Empire where Jews were allowed to live. It stretched from the Baltic Sea to the Black Sea.

"At the moment, we do. But you see, Uncle Binam thought of that. He left me enough money for the —"

The train turned a sharp corner and, for a moment, Liba was brought back to the present. Chaim stirred and mumbled something in his sleep; Liba patted him gently on the head and he settled back down.

Soon, Liba was lost in thought again. She remembered how she had run next door to tell Bayla all about Uncle Binam's will, how her parents had stayed up for hours, how they had spent the next few weeks planning and packing and arranging, how Mrs. Goldberg, Bayla's mother, had made endless amounts of fruit compote for the journey, so "the children shouldn't go hungry," and how amidst tears and best wishes, it had seemed that the entire town of Kelm had come to wish the Millers good-bye on the day of the family's departure.

Lost in these memories, Liba eventually drifted off to sleep, her head falling forward and her two thick braids coming to rest against Chaim's face.

Chapter Five

"I'm telling you, I heard him say a few words in Yiddish," insisted Hershel.

"I am sure you imagined it," said Peretz. "The driver is from here, from South Africa. You're tired from the train ride. Sometimes when you are really tired, you think you hear things, but you don't."

"Well, I also heard him say '*danke*' at the train station, when Tatty handed him our bags to put in the oxcart," continued Hershel.

"Be logical. We are in South Africa, not Russia. The people here speak English, like the man who checked our documents at the dock. How in the world would the driver know Yiddish?" asked Peretz.

"Maybe he took a trip once to Kelm and learned it, just like Mordke *di Amerikaner* learned English when he was in Cleveland," offered Chaim.

"I don't think so," said Peretz.

"Well, I do," countered Hershel.

The train had reached its last stop, the town of George, early that morning. Itzig had hired a driver to take the family on the final leg of their journey — north across the Outeniqua Mountains. The driver had spent the entire day carefully guiding his oxcart — a large, canvas-covered wagon pulled by a pair of oxen — over the Montagu Pass, the narrow road that twisted and wound its way through the mountains

The oxcart began its slow descent down the slopes to the valley below, where lay the town of Oudtshoorn. Liba listened half-heartedly to her brothers' conversation. She did not think the oxcart driver really spoke Yiddish, but as she had said to Peretz when they had first arrived, South Africa was a wonderful place, and anything was possible here.

Liba believed she already knew what the hotel looked like. Over the years, Uncle Binam had sent the family a number of postcards; Itzig had saved them in a small box in the kitchen. Liba had always enjoyed looking at these postcards, especially the one that had a photograph of a very big building situated on a generous plot of land, surrounded by tall trees and flowering bushes.

Ever since she had learned about Uncle Binam's property, Liba had become convinced that this was a photograph of his hotel. Bayla had agreed with her. *Why else would Uncle Binam have sent it?* both of them reasoned.

In the weeks leading up to the departure, Liba and Bayla talked endlessly about what it would be like to live in such a building, with its enormous roof, thick round columns, countless windows and wide front porch; to them it almost looked like a palace, where kings and queens might live. What impressed them the most was the fact that it was two stories tall. The only two-story building the girls had ever been inside was the *shul* in Kelm. The women's section was on the second floor, and was reached by a narrow wooden staircase.

Liba imagined herself in Uncle Binam's hotel, standing on a huge circular staircase, the type she had seen once in a newspaper. How much fun she and her brothers would have on those stairs, going around and around and up and down.

Down, down, down the oxcart went, all the way into the valley.

* ✻ *

Liba leaned forward, eager to see the hotel. A number of small stores were lined up on either side of the street; English letters were painted on the awnings that hung above their front doors. Up ahead, Liba could see a large, two-story building with a huge slanted roof. It looked just like the photograph on the postcard. "That's it! There's the hotel!" she shouted, barely able to contain her excitement.

"Where, Liba, where?" asked Chaim. "I can't see."

"Over there, you can't miss it! It has a huge window, right beside the ...," she began. But wait! The driver wasn't stopping. He continued to guide the cart along the street.

"Tatty! Tatty! Tell the driver to stop," Liba exclaimed. "He's going right past the hotel."

"Liba, I am sure he knows where he is going. He has the exact address. If he didn't stop, it means we are not there yet," replied Itzig.

"Oh," said Liba, disappointed. She turned to Chaim and said, "That wasn't the right building. I'll point it out to you as soon as I see it."

Liba kept her eyes focused on the street. She soon noticed a small white sign in the distance.

"That's it!" Liba shouts, barely able to contain her excitement.

Looking carefully, she thought she could see a few black letters. While on board the ship, she had tried to learn a little bit of English. She did her best now to read: *I – L – L*. She tried to sound the letters out, remembering that this was the way she had learned to read Hebrew, many years ago. The three letters spelled "ill." Oh! She knew that word. It meant "*krank*." When they had first boarded the ship, the boys had been very seasick. One of the English-speaking passengers had said that they looked "ill."

She noticed a few other letters: *H — O — T*. Oh! She knew this word, too. It meant "*heis*." When they had first arrived, one of the passengers had said to Mama that it was very hot here. *Ill and hot.* Liba wondered. *Hmm. What type of building could this be? Oh, yes, of course! It was obvious. Where did you go when you were ill and hot? To a hospital. They must be approaching the town's hospital.*

The oxcart began to slow down and before Liba knew what was happening, the driver stopped in front of the sign. *Why are we stopping at the hospital? Maybe the driver isn't feeling well? Maybe he is visiting someone?* The driver got down from his seat and came around to the side of the oxcart. Itzig now turned to the family and announced, "We're here! *Baruch Hashem*, we are here!"

Here? We are here? What was Tatty saying? There must be a mistake; the driver must have taken them to the wrong address. This wasn't a big, beautiful hotel. This was a long, narrow building, set amidst a jumbled mess of overgrown weeds. The two small windows that peered out onto the street were cracked, and there was a large gash in the front door. Liba looked at the sign again, more closely this time. Some of the letters were worn out and were very hard to see. She counted them. Twelve letters in all. She tried sounding them out, to make words. Was this possible? Was she reading the sign correctly? Liba's heart sank. The sign did not read "ILL" and "HOT." It read M**ILL**ER'S **HOT**EL. This was Uncle Binam's hotel.

Where was the wide front porch? The large windows? The second story? This is what Uncle Binam had given Tatty in his will? This was the palace? This is why they had left everybody and everything they knew and had come all this way?

Liba couldn't believe it.

Chapter Six

A wave of deep disappointment washed over Liba as she looked around the small lobby. Several tired-looking armchairs were scattered around the room; beneath them were a few old rugs, their pattern having faded long ago. An oil lamp dangled from the ceiling, its glass case cracked. A long wooden counter stood at the far right; behind it were a number of sagging wooden shelves, piled high with boxes. For a brief second, Liba imagined what would happen if the shelves suddenly snapped — the boxes would come crashing to the floor, their lids would fly off, and their contents would spill and scatter all over the lobby.

"Is anyone here?" Peretz asked the question that was on everyone's mind.

"There must be people here," said Itzig. "Remember, Uncle Binam mentioned the staff of the hotel."

"Then where are they?" asked Hershel.

"I don't know. I have an idea. Come with me."

Itzig approached the counter, his family following closely behind. He remembered reading somewhere that in certain places of business, if you rang a bell, a person came to your service. He looked around for a bell to ring, but he didn't find one. Instead, he tapped on the counter and waited. No one appeared. He tapped again, more forcefully this time.

A voice called out from somewhere, "I'm in the middle of something. I will be there in a minute."

"See?" said Peretz to Chaim. "Someone *is* here."

A small door to the right of the counter soon swung open and a young man appeared. He was tall and thin and had bright red hair and a small red beard; his green eyes were lively behind a pair of oval-shaped, wire-rimmed glasses.

"Hello, I do apologize. I did not hear you come in," he said, his tone pleasant.

"I am sorry to disturb you," said Itzig. He extended his hand and said, "My name is Itzig Miller."

The young man broke into a wide smile. He shook Itzig's hand and said, "*Bruchim haba'im*!

My name is Yom Tov Kessel. We have been expecting you! Wait here just a minute." He quickly disappeared down a long, narrow hallway.

"Where did he go?" Chaim whispered to Hershel.

"Maybe he went to find a friend of his," suggested Hershel.

"A friend of his? Here, at the hotel? I don't think so," said Peretz.

Yom Tov soon returned with a short, well-fed man wearing a pair of dark blue overalls.

"See, I told you he was going to get his friend," Hershel said to Peretz.

"*Shh*, boys," said their mama.

"I am Wolf Glick — porter, plumber, painter and wagon driver," the man said.

"Pleased to meet you, Mr. Glick," replied Itzig. "My name is Itzig Miller. This is my wife, Sorel, and our children."

"No, no, call me Wolf. Or you can call me Zev Wolf. But of course, if you insist, you may call me Mr. Glick, but really, that is much too formal, much too formal. When I think about it, almost no one ever calls me Mr. Glick, so I suggest you do

"Pleased to meet you," says Liba's father.

as everyone else does, and call me Wolf, unless, of course, you don't want to, in which case, I am happy for you to call me Mr. Glick."

"Perhaps you could show the family their rooms?" suggested Yom Tov. "I am sure they are anxious to unpack and get settled. I would do it myself, but at the moment, I am in the middle of something."

"Yes, yes, of course. Let me help you carry your bags," said Wolf. "Not all of the bags, that would be much too heavy, but one or two should be fine. No, actually, I believe I might be able to manage three, or four. Well, maybe not four. But three, certainly. Yes, I believe three is just right. I can carry two with my right hand and one with my left and then if I get tired in the middle, I can simply switch, unless of course you would like me to carry the samovar, in which case ..."

Liba sighed. She had a feeling this was going to take a long time.

* * *

Her suitcase almost completely unpacked, Liba stuck her hand in the small side pocket;

she touched something flat and smooth. It felt like paper. *What was it?* she wondered. *Oh,* she realized — *it was Bayla's letter*. Right before the Millers had left Kelm, just as they were about to drive away in the wagon, Bayla had come running toward them, waving a sheet of paper in her hand as if it were a flag. "Liba, Liba, you must take this with you," she had shouted.

"What is it?" Liba had called from her seat.

"Just a small note," Bayla had called back.

Itzig had asked the driver to wait just one more minute. Bayla dashed over to the wagon and thrust the piece of paper into her best friend's hand.

"I couldn't find an envelope. After all, when do I ever send letters to anyone?" Bayla said with a little smile, exposing the small gap between her two front teeth.

"That's fine. It's easier for me to read this way," said Liba.

"No, I don't want you to read it until you reach Ooo ... Oa ..." Bayla could not pronounce the name of the town. "Until you get to your uncle's fancy hotel," she finished. "Fold it up and put it in a safe place until then."

Liba and Bayla had hugged each other one last time, and the wagon soon pulled away.

I guess Bayla would want me to read it now, Liba thought, *even though Uncle Binam's hotel isn't as "fancy" as Bayla and I had imagined. How long has it been since I last saw her? Four weeks? Five weeks? It was hard to remember.*

Liba sat down on the small narrow bed in the room and carefully unfolded the letter.

Dear Liba,

I wanted to tell you how much I miss you! Of course, I am writing this while you are still here, right next door, but I know that when you read this, you will have been gone a very long time! I hope no one in your family got seasick on the ship.

I know that you must be having a wonderful time all the way over there in South Africa. I am sure the hotel is even more beautiful than it looked on that postcard. Does it really have two floors? Do you get to sleep on the second floor? Is it scary to sleep so high up? Do you speak English yet? Have you made any new friends?

Write me back soon. When I get your

letter, I will show it to my parents, just like we planned. Once they see how wonderful everything is over there, maybe they really will want to move there, too. After all, my tatty always says there's no future for us Jews here in Russia.

Say hi to your brothers. Also, say hi to your mama and tatty.

Love, your very best friend,

Bayla Goldberg

P.S. Are you happy now with what you have, Liba? You must be, now that you're living in a palace.

Liba smiled sadly as she remembered the Shabbos afternoon when she and Bayla had studied that *mishnah* in *Pirkei Avos*. She missed her best friend very much, and she desperately wanted to write her back, but how could she? How could Liba tell her that although the country was beautiful, the hotel was dark, dusty and run down? That it looked absolutely nothing like the photograph on Uncle Binam's postcard? That Liba had no idea how her mama and tatty were going to make a living because it seemed like no one had stayed in the hotel for years? Sudden tears formed in Liba's eyes.

We had so many plans! As soon as we were settled, and Mama and Tatty had started to work at the hotel, I was going to ask them if they could use a few extra helpers. I was so certain that such a big hotel could always use more staff. Then, I was going to suggest that they write Bayla's parents, the Goldbergs, and invite them to come to Oudtshoorn, to work in the hotel. When they arrived, we would help them find a nice place to live nearby, and Bayla and I could be neighbors again. This is what we had talked about, for hours, ever since that summer night when Mama and Tatty had told me that we were moving to South Africa ....

"What you need is a nice bowl of mushroom-barley soup," said a woman's voice.

Liba looked up, startled.

"Mushroom-barley soup. It's delicious," added the woman.

Liba looked at the woman. She was tall, with a kind face and light blue eyes set under dark eyebrows. She wore a simple kerchief on her head, and a blue and white checked dress that fell to her ankles.

"I'm sorry. D-did y-you say something about soup?" Liba stammered.

"Yes, mushroom-barley soup. It works wonders. Allow me to introduce myself. My name is Mrs. Ziesel Glick. I believe you have already met my husband, Mr. Wolf Glick."

Liba nodded.

"I have been the cook at Miller's Hotel for almost fifteen years, ever since Wolf and I arrived from Plungen, a town not too far from Kelm. I've seen it all — happy travelers, disappointed travelers, excited travelers, anxious travelers. What's good for all of them, I always say, is a nice bowl of mushroom-barley soup. So come along. The rest of your family is already in the dining room. We don't want them to eat it all before you get there, do we?"

"Uh, uh, no, I guess not," said Liba, slowly standing up.

"I'll show you the way," said the woman.

Drying her eyes with the sleeve of her dress, Liba followed the woman out of the room.

Chapter Seven

Mrs. Glick thanked the woman behind the counter and left the store. Liba and her brothers followed closely behind and stepped out onto the street known as "*Der Yiddishe Gass*" — The Jewish Street. Mrs. Glick had explained that this street stretched thirty miles, from the town of Oudtshoorn all the way to the neighboring town of Calitzdorp. All the shops — over twenty in total — were owned by Jewish people. There was even a boarding house here that had a *sefer Torah* and daily *minyanim*, she told them proudly.

Mrs. Glick knew that Itzig and Sorel were going to be very busy today. With her husband's help, they planned to inspect each room of the hotel and make a list of everything that needed to be repaired or replaced; this was going to be a very long list. Over breakfast, she had offered to take Liba and the boys with her on her errands.

"I need your help," she told them. "I will have a lot to carry. I want to buy a few pounds of flour, and sugar and some cocoa and a bit of cinnamon. I want to make *kipferl.* They are Mr. Glick's favorite pastry. At least, they might be. The last time I made them, he said, 'Thank you, dear, these are my favorite,' but the next night, when I served him a few honey cookies, he said, 'Thank you, dear, *these* are my favorite,' and then just two nights ago, when I served him *mohn* cookies, he said, 'Thank you, dear, *these* are my favorite' — so I am not sure."

Liba and her brothers had smiled, listening to Mrs. Glick's re-telling. Although they had just met Mr. Glick yesterday, they could easily imagine him saying this.

As they continued along *Der Yiddishe Gass,* Liba tried to read the English words she saw painted on all the signs. They soon passed a small red brick building. A large wooden sign hanging high above the front door read, "David Berg, Ostrich Feather Buyer." Liba read the first two words fairly easily, but she struggled to read the third one. "O…O…ssstt…" *Oh, it is that word again! Mama had said it was some kind of big bird. Is this man selling these birds? Why?*

"Mrs. Glick, what is an *oosstrichhh*?"

"An ostrich?"

"Yes, that's it. When we arrived in South Africa, people kept saying that word when we told them we were going to Oudtshoorn. We just passed a store that sells them."

Mrs. Glick chuckled. "No, my dear. They do not sell ostriches here. They sell their feathers."

"Who sells the feathers?" asked Peretz, becoming interested in the conversation.

"Many, many people," replied Mrs. Glick. "Ostrich feathers are big business here in Oudtshoorn, especially for Jews."

"What do they do with the feathers?" asked Chaim. "Do they make featherbeds with them, like Mama does?"

"No, my boy. Ostrich feathers are far too valuable for that. People pay money — lots of money — for ostrich feathers. All the fancy ladies in Paris and Vienna wear them as boas — scarves — and they wear them in their hats, too."

"How did the Jews in Oudtshoorn become involved in selling ostrich feathers?" Peretz asked, as they turned a corner.

"That is an excellent question and it deserves an excellent answer. I can't tell you the whole story now, while I am walking along the street carrying packages. Let's wait until later, until we can have a cold glass of milk and a nice slice of my delicious *babka*."

"Aww," said Hershel, sounding disappointed. "It was getting so interesting. Now we have to wait until we get all the way back to the hotel."

"Oh, I know," said Chaim. "Look, over there. There's a bench. Mrs. Glick, we could go there and sit down. We could put the packages down, too, and you could tell us all about it."

"Please, Mrs. Glick?" begged Hershel.

"All right, boys," she agreed.

Mrs. Glick led everybody across the street. They all sat down and Mrs. Glick put the packages down beside her.

"Now, where were we?" she asked.

"You were about to tell us how the Jews here became involved in the ostrich feather business," said Peretz.

"Oh, yes. You see, many years ago, when the Jews first started arriving here, many of them worked as peddlers. The farmers here called

"Many years ago ...," Mrs. Glick begins.

them *'smouse,'* the Dutch word for peddlers. The *smouse* traveled far out into the countryside with their goods, trying to sell whatever they could — buttons, mirrors, pots, pans, candles, socks. They would walk for hours and hours in the heat, their heavy leather bags slung over their shoulders. When they became tired, they would take a nap by the side of the road."

"Mama would never, ever let me do that," said Chaim. "I'd get my pants all dirty. Especially around here. The roads are so dusty," he added.

"*Oy*, Chaim!" said Hershel. "These peddlers were grown-ups. Their mamas weren't telling them what to do anymore."

"I guess you're right," said the little boy.

Mrs. Glick smiled at Chaim and continued. "Once a *smous* had worked for a while and managed to save some money, he would buy a donkey. When he had a bit more money, he bought a horse and cart. Later, he often bought a small store. A number of Jewish men still work as *smouse* today. Years ago, some of them used to stay with us at Miller's Hotel. We had a special room at the front where they could store their goods overnight. Not anymore, though."

Liba would have liked to ask Mrs. Glick why the *smouse* — or anyone else, it seemed — no longer stayed at Uncle Binam's hotel, but she decided it was not the right time for this question.

"Some farms the *smouse* visited were ostrich farms, here in this area. The farmers raised ostriches for their feathers and for their meat. The *smouse* would trade some of their goods for these feathers, and over time, some of the *smouse* became ostrich feather buyers and dealers. I have heard people say that today there are over 250 licensed feather buyers in the area, almost all of them Jews."

"Where are all the ostriches?" asked Peretz.

"On ostrich farms."

"Could we go to one of these farms, to see the ostriches?" asked Hershel.

"Could we? Could we?" Chaim and Hershel asked at the same time.

Mrs. Glick thought this over. "Maybe one day, but we couldn't walk there. The farms are outside of Oudtshoorn."

Noticing the look of disappointment on the boys' faces, she quickly added, "We certainly could take a walk another day to see the feather palaces. I am sure you would like that. They are not that far from here."

"Feather palaces? Houses made of feathers? Don't they blow away when it's windy?" asked Chaim.

Mrs. Glick laughed. "They are called feather palaces because they are huge houses built with money made from dealing in ostrich feathers. The houses are made from sandstone, a stone that is found all over the area. It is very pretty. I must admit, the color of the stone always reminds me of cheese blintzes."

Something suddenly occurred to Liba. "Are these 'feather palaces' two stories tall, with big wide porches and iron gates, surrounded by big trees?" she asked.

"Exactly. Did you drive past one of them on your way to the hotel yesterday?"

"Yes, I think so. And our Uncle Binam sent us a photograph of one, once. It looked so beautiful, almost like a palace. My best friend Bayla and I used to stare at that photograph for hours." Liba was too embarrassed to tell Mrs. Glick that she had mistakenly thought it was a photograph of the hotel.

"That doesn't surprise me; they are very impressive-looking. The first feather palace was built about seven years ago. A few more are built every year. I remember your uncle used to go and watch them being put up; he found it very interesting. That was before the new … well … never mind."

Standing up quickly, she said, "We must be getting back. I want to have these *kipferl* ready for tonight, and the dough needs a few hours to rise."

Mrs. Glick led everyone back to the hotel. As soon as they reached the front door, the boys dashed inside, shouting.

"Mama, Mrs. Glick said maybe one day we can visit an ostrich farm!"

"Maybe we can see a feather palace one day! Would you like to go with us, Tatty? They don't blow away, don't worry. They aren't really made of feathers."

Liba stopped to do up the buckle on her right shoe. As she bent down, she thought she saw the figure of a man dart from the back of the hotel. She straightened up to take a second look. *No, there's no one there,* she thought. *I must have imagined it.*

"Come inside. Mama wants you," Chaim shouted from the front door.

Liba hurried into the hotel, immediately forgetting all about the man she thought she had seen.

Chapter Eight

"I'm telling you, I heard him say *'fenster,'*" insisted Hershel, as he pulled another weed out of the ground.

"Oh, Hershel, not again! We have been through this a hundred times! You keep thinking that everyone in Oudtshoorn speaks Yiddish, but it's impossible. We're in South Africa now, remember? The official language here is English." Peretz threw a weed into the bucket at his feet.

"I am sure of it. Right before we came outside, I heard Tatty talking to that man with the bushy beard. The man pointed to the cracked front window and said *'fenster.'*"

"Do you know what I think?" Peretz asked Hershel.

"What?" Hershel continued weeding and didn't look up. He was not entirely certain he wanted to know.

"I think that maybe, just maybe,

you are a little bit homesick. And maybe, just maybe, this is the reason you keep thinking you hear South Africans speak Yiddish."

"No, that's not it. Not at all," said Hershel.

"Do you want to know what *I* think?" asked Chaim, who had been listening to the conversation as he sat on the ground and filled a hole using a small shovel.

Hershel and Peretz exchanged quick smiles. "Sure, Chaim, tell us," said Peretz.

Brushing the dirt from his pants, Chaim got to his feet. In as grown-up a voice as possible, he said, "Let's go ask Yom Tov Kessel, or Mr. or Mrs. Glick. They would know. After all, they have lived in Oudtshoorn a long time. If they say South Africans speak Yiddish, then they do. If they say they don't, then they don't."

"That's a good idea," said Peretz.

"Why not? I'm getting tired of all this weeding, anyway," agreed Hershel.

BEEP. BEEP. BEEP.

The brothers looked up and saw a car driving toward them.

"Oh! Oh! Look. Another one! Another one! It's coming toward us!" shouted Chaim, jumping up and down and pointing down the street.

"Can you see? There are two men inside — a driver and someone else," said Hershel.

"Oh! I know! They are two friends taking a trip together, and they want to stay at the hotel," exclaimed Chaim. "Our very first guests! I can't wait to tell Liba!"

"Maybe," said Peretz. "Let's see."

The car pulled up in front of the hotel. The driver, wearing a dark suit and matching cap, opened the door and got out. He walked around to the other side of the car and held the door open. A second man stepped out. Chaim noticed he had a long narrow nose and a sharp pointy chin. His eyes were small and dark, almost black. *Back home in Kelm, the crows that used to land on his mama's clothesline had the same kind of eyes*, Chaim thought.

"I am looking for Mr. Itzig Miller," said the man. "Do you know where I may find him?"

The boys understood that the man was looking for their tatty. Peretz nodded and motioned for the man to follow him into the hotel. Once inside, Peretz led him to the front desk. Yom Tov Kessel was not there.

"I am looking for Mr. Itzig Miller.
Do you know where I may find him?"

"Mr. Kessel, there is someone here," Peretz called. There was no answer.

Peretz tapped on the counter and waited. Yom Tov Kessel did not appear. Peretz tapped a second time. After a minute or so, a familiar voice called, "I'm in the middle of something. I will be there in a minute."

Yom Tov Kessel soon appeared.

"Hello," he said to the man in English. "How may I help you?"

"Are you Mr. Miller, the owner?"

"No, sir, Yom Tov Kessel is my name. Do you wish to speak with the owner?"

"Yes. Immediately."

Yom Tov turned to the boys. "Your tatty is in the kitchen," he told them in Yiddish. "Go get him at once."

The boys would have loved to have gone back outside to admire the car, but they could tell from the look on Yom Tov's face that this might be important business. They hurried to the kitchen, where they found their tatty and Mr. Glick replacing a floorboard.

"Tatty! Come quickly! A man with a motor-car wants to see you!" Hershel shouted.

Itzig looked up from his crouched position and asked, “A man with a motorcar? Here? Wants to see me? Wolf, do you have any idea what this might be about?”

Tossing a few nails back and forth between his hands, Wolf said, “No, Itzig, I am sorry, I don’t. I mean, I don’t think I do. I suppose, if I thought about it, I might have an idea, but then, Hershel said you should come quickly, so at the moment, I don’t think I have time for one, but perhaps later, when we do have some time, I might come up with an idea, that is, if you still want one then.”

“That’s all right, Wolf,” said Itzig, straightening up.

“Sorel?” he asked his wife, who was standing at the kitchen table. She, Mrs. Glick and Liba had been rolling out dough to make *lokshen*. “Do you know anything about this?”

Sorel gave her head a small shake. She didn’t know, either.

Everyone followed Itzig into the lobby. The man was still standing at the front desk, a look of boredom on his face. Itzig introduced himself and stuck out his hand.

The man ignored Itzig's hand. Instead, he drew in a loud breath, as if preparing to deliver a speech. "My name is Mr. Lionel Minty. I am the assistant to the chief inspector, Regulations and Standards Division, the Ministry of Public Works, the Union of South Africa."

Itzig shot Yom Tov a quick look. He had not understood a word. Yom Tov began to translate from English into Yiddish.

"It has come to my attention that Miller's Hotel, presently owned by Mr. Itzig Miller, located at 15 Albert Street, Oudtshoorn, is in violation of the following building regulations: 7, 62, 81 and 89. A building is defined as any structure, be it of a permanent or a temporary nature, irrespective of the materials used in the construction thereof, used for or in connection with a) the accommodation or convenience of human beings, or b) the manufacture, processing, storage, display or sale of any goods, or c) the rendering of any service, or d) any part thereof, as defined in paragraph a) b) or c). Any facilities or system, or part or portion thereof, within or outside but incidental to a building —"

Yom Tov coughed. Mr. Minty paused to look at him.

"I am sorry, sir, but I am having difficulty understanding you. I am afraid I am unable to translate properly."

Mr. Minty's small dark eyes grew smaller and darker as a look of annoyance passed across his face.

"Fine. It's like this. There are lots of problems with this place. Lots. It was built without a permit. The truss, that is, the roof, is crooked. The structure is too low and does not allow for proper drainage. And finally, this building is unsightly and objectionable."

"Unsightly? Objectionable?" asked Yom Tov, unfamiliar with these words.

"Ugly. The place is ugly."

With difficulty, Yom Tov translated Mr. Minty's words into Yiddish.

Itzig's face grew pale. In a low voice, he said, "Tell him that I am truly sorry. I didn't know. We will do our very best to fix these problems as soon as possible."

Yom Tov relayed the message. Mr. Minty gave a quick toss of his head. "I'm afraid it's far too late in the day for that. In accordance with subsection 10–1 of the Regulations and Standards Division, the Ministry of Public Works, the Union of South Africa, any building, as defined as any structure, be it of a permanent or temporary — "

Yom Tov coughed again. Mr. Minty paused a second time. "The point is, this building is to be destroyed exactly thirty days from now, on January 27, 1911."

"Destroyed?" asked Yom Tov.

"Thirty days?" asked Mrs. Glick.

"January 27, 1911?" asked Mr. Glick.

"Yes, it is all here in writing." Mr. Minty reached into the pocket of his jacket and took out an envelope. He handed it to Itzig. Before anyone had a chance to ask him any questions, he was gone. A few seconds later, the sounds of a car starting and then driving away could be heard from the street outside.

Itzig sank into a nearby chair. Though he hadn't understood everything Mr. Minty had said, he had understood enough.

Chapter Nine

Liba and her family sat in the lobby and listened as Mr. and Mrs. Glick and Yom Tov told them more of the story of Miller's Hotel.

"Fifteen years ago this week, in fact," said Mrs. Glick. "I remember it well. Wolf and I were married only a few months, and we arrived here in Oudtshoorn. A distant cousin of mine had written me a letter, encouraging us to come. But by the time we arrived, she had decided she didn't like the weather and she had moved to Manchester, England. We didn't speak the language, we didn't know anyone and we didn't have enough money for return tickets. Who was it who welcomed us, helped us?"

"Yom Tov Kessel?" Hershel offered.

"No, my boy, not Yom Tov; he arrived many years later. It was Binam Miller, your Uncle Binam, *zichrono livracha*. We first met him in a bakery, on *Der Yiddishe Gass.*"

"We were looking to buy a black bread. Or was it a rye? Yes, I believe it was a rye, a double rye, actually. I think. No, wait, it was a marble rye. That is why I am confused. Yes, a marble rye." Mr. Glick added, "You know, the type with all the swirls."

Mrs. Glick continued. "Binam took us in, gave us a place to live and offered both of us jobs." With a sad look on her face, she continued. "He worked so hard, all those years. He wanted everything to be just right so that his guests would be comfortable. No, more than just comfortable — he wanted them to feel as if they were at home."

"And a few years later, he hired me," added Yom Tov.

"Did he meet you at a bakery, too?" asked Hershel.

Yom Tov smiled and said, "No, I met Binam when I stayed here once, overnight."

"Did you stay in our room?" asked Chaim. "Were you the one who broke our nightstand?"

"Chaim!" said Sorel. "That isn't a very nice question."

Yom Tov laughed and said, "No, Chaim, I'm

afraid that happened later. I was working as a *smous* but I was very unhappy. I was not cut out for it. I had come here from the small town of Keydan, as a teenager. I had big dreams of striking it rich, starting as a *smous* and eventually opening my very own store, but I quickly found out that the life of a *smous* — the sun, the heat and all that walking — wasn't for me. Binam offered me a job. He said he needed someone at the front desk to welcome the guests, to make sure everyone was happy, to see to all their needs."

Mr. Glick shook his head sadly. "And to think they want to knock the hotel down. It is so hard to imagine. I mean, I *can* imagine, they would use some sort of wrecking ball and the roof would begin to crack and then crumple and finally collapse, and the windows would shatter and break into tiny pieces and glass shards would fly everywhere, and the walls would shift and shake and tumble to the ground, and then there would be a huge heap of rubble and broken glass all over, so actually, I *can* imagine, but it is hard to believe. I mean, I can believe it, because I was just here now when that Mr. Minty told us that the hotel is in violation of building regulations 7, 62, 81 and 89."

"Those days were so busy," Yom Tov continued. "Sometimes every room was booked and we actually had to turn people away. Believe it or not, travelers would reserve a room in the hotel from one year to the next. I kept track of it all, in a big book I kept right behind the counter. But then, a few years ago, everything changed."

"Why? What changed?" Liba blurted.

"The Royal Crown. That's what changed everything," said Yom Tov sadly.

"The Royal Crown?" asked Sorel. "What is that?"

"It was a brand new hotel, a 'luxury' hotel, they called it. Just up the street from here. Thick carpets in every room, fine linen imported from Egypt on each bed, beautiful paintings hanging on all the walls and, believe it or not, washrooms inside each and every hotel room."

"Washrooms inside each and every hotel room?" repeated Hershel. "Oh, my!"

"People started staying there instead of staying here with us. At first, Binam wasn't worried. He knew the Royal Crown was a much fancier hotel, but he also knew that the owner didn't live there. He lived far away in Cape Town. He didn't greet each person every morning with a smile, he didn't make sure the cook prepared everyone's favorite foods, he didn't have a few games and toys set aside for the children; well, it just wasn't the same."

Yom Tov continued. "A few years ago, a man approached Binam. I remember it clearly. Binam and I were standing outside at the time. The man offered to buy the hotel, but Binam refused. The man said, 'Miller, you're a fool. You will never get a better offer. Never.'"

"I completely understand why Uncle Binam didn't want to sell the hotel. It was his home," said Itzig.

"No, it was more than that," said Yom Tov. "He always said, 'I want Itzig and his family to have this one day.' He remembered how hard life was back in Russia — the Czar's ever-changing rules and restrictions, the pogroms, the poverty. There were so many times that he wanted to write and tell you to come, but he kept waiting for business to improve. 'Next month,' he'd say, 'next month I'll tell Itzig to come,' but he never did. The three of us tried to help, to make a little extra money. Wolf took on odd jobs as a handyman, Ziesel sold some of her baked goods, and I started working on my … well, never mind. But business never picked up. And then, Binam took ill, and … " Yom Tov's voice trailed off.

In a voice so low it was almost a whisper, Itzig said, "He kept this hotel for me? He had a chance to sell it and held on to it for me, for my family?"

"Yes," said Mrs. Glick, her voice breaking.

Sorel took out a handkerchief and handed it to Mrs. Glick.

"We will not let the hotel be destroyed," stated Itzig, his voice firm.

"What will we do, Tatty?" asked Peretz.

"I don't know. With Hashem's help, I will think of something. But for now, there is to be no more talk of this matter. It is almost Shabbos, and we must prepare."

"We will not let the hotel be destroyed,"
Itzig says determinedly.

Chapter Ten

"Are you ready?" Yom Tov called from his perch at the front of the wagon.

"Of course. We've been ready for hours!" shouted Chaim.

"Wonderful! And what are you ready for?" Yom Tov called.

"For our special surprise adventure!" all three boys shouted at once.

"Then let's go!" Yom Tov flicked the reins of the horse and they were off.

Although everyone had tried to enjoy Shabbos, the mood in the hotel was grim; it was impossible to forget what Mr. Minty had told them late Friday afternoon. On Motzei Shabbos, after Itzig had made Havdalah, Yom Tov had offered to take the children on 'a special surprise adventure' in the morning. He hoped that this would cheer them up.

"I know what the surprise is," offered Chaim from his seat in the wagon. Trying his best to sound as if he had already turned six, and wasn't still five, he said, "We're going to see a talking mountain."

"A talking mountain? There's no such thing. That's ridiculous," said Hershel. "I think we're going to see one of those feather palaces, those big fancy houses."

"No, we wouldn't need a wagon for that," said Peretz, matter-of-factly. "Mrs. Glick said those houses weren't far from the hotel, that we could walk there one day."

"Maybe we're going to buy a few more groceries for Mrs. Glick?" offered Chaim, trying to come up with a suggestion that his brothers wouldn't find quite as ridiculous as his first one.

"That wouldn't be much of a special surprise adventure," said Hershel, shaking his head.

Peretz looked at Liba and asked, "What do you think?"

Liba didn't answer.

"Liba, what do you think?" he asked a second time.

"About what?"

"About the special surprise adventure. What do you think we are going to do?" Peretz asked.

Liba was too busy thinking about what her tatty was doing today to think about where Yom Tov was taking them. Itzig had gone with Mr. Glick to speak with a few of the Jewish men in Oudtshoorn who had lived in the town for a long time. These men knew a few important people in Cape Town. Itzig hoped that one of them could give him the name of someone there who might help him. *What will happen if Tatty is not successful?* Liba wondered. *What will we do? Where will we live? Will we go back to Kelm? Do we even have enough money left for return tickets? And what about Mr. and Mrs. Glick, and Yom Tov? What will happen to them?*

"Oh, I don't know, something nice," Liba replied distractedly.

All the boys looked at their sister in amazement. She always had such exciting ideas and suggestions. Didn't she even want to guess where they were going?

Yom Tov suddenly brought the wagon to a stop. He got down from his perch and walked toward a large wooden gate. "We're almost there!" he cried as he opened it. He then got back into the wagon and continued driving for a few more minutes. A sprawling, iron-roofed house with a huge pillar on either side soon came into view. Yom Tov pulled up in front of a cluster of blue gum trees.

"Here we are!" he announced as he stepped down. "This is the home of a good friend of mine, Mr. Cornelius Kruger."

The boys happily tumbled out of the wagon. Liba followed. Yom Tov guided everyone to the front of the house and up a few wooden stairs. He knocked on the door; a man with a large, weather-beaten face soon appeared. He was wearing dark green pants, a worn shirt and a battered straw hat.

The man greeted Yom Tov warmly and they stood and chatted. After a few minutes, Yom Tov turned to the children and said, "Mr. Kruger welcomes you and says that he is pleased to meet you. He will take you out to the back now, to the lake."

"Oh! Oh! We are going swimming!" Chaim shouted. "I love swimming. There was a tiny stream near our house, back in Kelm, and when it was very hot, Mama used to take us there sometimes."

"We are not going swimming, Chaim. Definitely not," said Yom Tov, a playful look on his face.

Mr. Kruger picked up a nearby bucket and led everyone along a narrow, winding path that led away from the side of the house. As they walked, Hershel and Peretz resumed the argument they had been having ever since they had arrived in South Africa.

"I'm telling you, I just heard him now, when he was talking to Yom Tov. He said lots of Yiddish words — '*kinder*' (children), '*gut*' (good) and '*kum*' (come)," insisted Hershel.

"Oh, not this again! The man is a South African farmer! He's probably lived here his whole life. Where would he possibly have learned Yiddish?" asked Peretz.

"I don't know where. But I heard him. I did." Turning to Chaim, Hershel asked, "Didn't you hear it, too?"

"Yes, I did. I mean, no, I didn't, except that maybe I did, a little," Chaim replied, not wanting to find himself in the middle of an argument.

"You know what I am going to do right now?"

asked Hershel. Not waiting for a reply, he continued, "I am going to ask Yom Tov if the man was speaking Yiddish."

"Fine. But don't be surprised when he starts laughing at you," said Peretz.

Hershel approached Yom Tov and told him about the disagreement the two brothers had been having. Yom Tov listened carefully and then smiled.

Noticing the smile, Peretz said to Hershel, "See? He thinks your question is silly. I told you so."

"No, not exactly, Peretz," said Yom Tov.

"Hershel is right?" asked Peretz in a loud voice, sounding shocked. "How could that be?"

Yom Tov stopped walking and turned to face the children. "Let me explain. Hundreds of years ago, many people from Holland settled here. At that time, the area was known as 'the Cape.' They spoke a type of Dutch that was very similar to German. Over time, these people added words from the languages spoken by the people around them. Eventually, this language came to be called Afrikaans. The people who spoke it were called Afrikaaners, though sometimes they were called Boers. It continues to be spoken by many thousands of people today. The official language of the country is English, and this is the main language you will be taught once you start school. However, most — if not all — of the farmers speak Afrikaans, and it is very likely that you will be taught this language in school, too. Many Jews have learned to speak it, to be able to talk to the Afrikaaners."

"That was the language you were speaking just now, to Mr. Kruger?" asked Peretz.

"Yes, it was. I had to learn Afrikaans when I was working as a *smous*, so I could communicate with the farmers. Now, you may not know this, but Yiddish is also very similar to German, although, of course, it is written with Hebrew letters. So, there are in fact quite a few words in Afrikaans that are similar to Yiddish. What Hershel has heard are some of those words. The longer you live here, the more words like this you will notice. Words like '*boom*' in Afrikaans, and '*baum*' in Yiddish (tree), and '*middag*' in Afrikaans, and '*mitag*' (afternoon) in Yiddish. So, you see, Hershel is a little bit right, and you, Peretz, are also a little bit right."

"That is exactly what I was trying to say," said Chaim proudly.

Hershel and Peretz looked at each other in amazement. They had never both been right at the same time; they didn't know how to respond.

Mr. Kruger stopped walking. They had reached a small lake. "Keep your eyes on the water, now," advised Yom Tov. "It is feeding time."

Before anyone had a chance to ask what "feeding time" meant, Mr. Kruger stuck his right hand into the bucket and pulled out several dead fish. He threw them into the water. Nothing happened for a second, but then ... One! Two! Three! Four! Five huge dark green creatures covered in thick scaly hides jumped out of the water. Their enormous jaws snapped repeatedly and clamped down on the fish, exposing two incredible rows of pointy teeth that locked together perfectly.

"*AHHH!*" shrieked Chaim. "Sea monsters! Sea monsters!" He burst into tears and buried his head in the folds of Liba's skirt.

Mr. Kruger stuck his hand into the bucket a second time and threw more fish into the water. The creatures continued to jump and snap and clamp.

"*Ahhh!*" shrieks Chaim.
"Sea monsters! Sea monsters!"

"What … what … what … are those …?" Peretz asked weakly.

"Why, they're crocodiles," said Yom Tov calmly.

"Croco … what?" asked Hershel.

"Crocodiles. Huge, lizard-like creatures. This is a crocodile farm. They live here in this lake, but they can be found all over South Africa. These crocodiles aren't even fully grown yet. They can grow up to be fifteen to twenty feet long and weigh hundreds and hundreds of pounds. They eat everything — fish, insects, animals. This makes them very dangerous. You must never get too close to one."

Yom Tov suddenly took a small notebook and a pencil from the pocket of his shirt.

"What is that, Yom Tov?" asked Hershel.

"This, oh, it's just a little book I like to take with me when I visit the crocodile farm."

"What do you do with it?" asked Peretz.

"Oh, well, I …" Yom Tov noticed that Mr. Kruger was sticking his hand into the bucket again. "I'll tell you about it another time. Get ready. Mr. Kruger is about to throw some more fish into the lake."

The crocodiles jumped and snapped and clamped again. Yom Tov quickly sketched something in his notebook and then put it back in his pocket.

Mr. Kruger now showed everyone that the bucket was empty; feeding time was over. With Yom Tov working as a translator, he told them a bit about the crocodiles, and then Mr. Kruger led everyone to the front of the house. He and Yom Tov chatted for a few more minutes; Liba and the boys now understood that the two men were speaking Afrikaans.

Everyone soon climbed back into the wagon. Yom Tov returned to his perch at the front and flicked the reins. The horse began to trot. It was only then that Chaim — who had clung to Liba's skirt ever since first setting sight on the crocodiles — dared to look up. "That was great! Let's come back here tomorrow!" he suggested.

Chapter Eleven

"Tatty, Mama, where are you? We have to tell you all about it! Yom Tov took us to see the most incredible creatures!" Hershel shouted as he ran into the lobby of the hotel.

"They're called crocodiles! They look like monsters! They are huge, and they have these big long tails and four short little legs, but they also know how to swim, so they don't need to use their legs that much, only if they really want to," called Chaim, following closely behind.

"The man there, Mr. Kruger, told us crocodiles have sixty-eight teeth. When one breaks and falls out, another just grows in its place. Isn't that amazing?" added Peretz.

Itzig and Sorel were seated side by side in the lobby. They were busy talking to each other and did not look up.

Mrs. Glick suddenly appeared, a smudge of flour on her nose. "Boys! What perfect timing. I just took my apple strudel out of the oven. Come with me and you'll each have a slice, and you'll tell me all about your adventure."

"While we're eating, we can pretend to be crocodiles," Chaim said, opening and closing his mouth wide, exposing two rows of tiny, perfect baby teeth.

"Right! Like this!" Hershel demonstrated, opening his mouth and doing exactly as Chaim had done.

"That's disgusting, Hershel. Stop that," said Peretz.

"You didn't say it was disgusting when Chaim did it," protested Hershel.

Mrs. Glick gently ushered the boys into the kitchen.

Liba approached her parents. "Tatty, what happened at the meeting?" she asked quietly.

Her tatty didn't answer. He simply shook his head.

"Tatty met with two Jewish men, Mr. Jaff and Mr. Freedman," said her mama. "Both of them are well-respected, successful businessmen here in Oudtshoorn. They were very pleasant and sincerely wanted to help, but they said that, unfortunately, there is nothing they can do."

"But didn't Mr. Glick tell you that these men know a few important people in Cape Town? Was he wrong?"

"No," said her tatty, slowly. "Mr. Glick was right. Both men know a few government officials from Cape Town. That is not the problem. The problem is that just a few months ago, everything changed here in South Africa."

"What do you mean?" asked Liba.

"The men explained to Tatty that this past May, after four years of discussions, the British government united four separate colonies — the Cape of Good Hope, the Natal, the Transvaal and the Orange Free State — into one large country," her mama replied.

"Mama, I don't understand. What does this have to do with finding someone who might help us?"

"You see, the country known as the Union of South Africa has officially only existed for eight months. The very first national election was held only three months ago, in September," explained her mama.

Liba was trying her best to understand what

this meant, but it didn't make any sense.

"None of the people who work for the government — Mr. Minty, for instance — has been in his position for very long. No one, including the men I met today, knows them yet," said Itzig.

Liba fiddled with the ribbon on her right braid and thought this over for a minute. "Did they offer you any advice, Tatty?"

"Yes, they did. They suggested I write a letter — that is, someone should help me write a letter, in English, to Mr. Minty — and try to explain our situation: that we have just arrived, that I have a wife and four young children to provide for, and that I came here all the way from Russia, believing I would be able to make a living from my uncle's hotel, and that, well, that I have no other options."

"Would that work?" Liba asked.

"*Oy*, Liba'le, we don't know, but we have to try," her mama said sadly.

"I will go and ask Yom Tov right now if he can help Tatty write the letter," said Liba. She hurried to the front desk but Yom Tov wasn't there. She was surprised. They had just returned from the crocodile farm a little while ago. Where could he have gone? Liba called his name, but there was no answer. She tapped on the counter and waited. Then she called his name again.

"Just a minute. I am in the middle of something," a familiar voice called back. *In the middle of something, now? Why is he always 'in the middle of something'? The middle of what, exactly?* Liba wondered.

Yom Tov appeared, patting the pocket of his shirt. Liba thought she could see the notebook peeking out the top. "I am sorry to keep you waiting, Liba. I was just looking at what I had … well, never mind. It isn't important right now. May I help you?"

"I hope so," she said.

Liba held the envelope tightly in her right hand; the penny was in her left. She was on her way to mail the letter Yom Tov had helped her tatty write yesterday. Mrs. Glick had told her to look for a tall building with a large white sign that spelled POST OFFICE in black letters. Liba was fairly certain she would have no difficulty finding the building; her English had improved a lot in the short time the family had been in Oudtshoorn.

Liba was to use the penny to buy a stamp. Neither Mr. Glick, Mrs. Glick, nor Yom Tov had mailed a letter in a long time, but Mr. Glick had said that this was the right amount —or so Liba thought he had said.

"As far as I can remember, which of course isn't all that far, having lived here for only fifteen years, whereas others have lived here much longer, but it is not really all that near, either, when you think about it, because others, like yourselves, have just recently arrived, it has always cost one penny to mail a letter. A letter, mind you — not a package, nor a parcel, nor anything heavy, awkward or unusual — and of course, I am speaking of a letter sent to Cape Town only, not Paris or Kansas or Caracas or anywhere else, at least as far as I know, which, as I have said, isn't really all that far, though it might be considered far, by some people, in certain situations."

As she walked along the street, Liba thought about the letter Bayla had written her. She felt badly that she had not written back; she easily could imagine Bayla asking her mother,

Mrs. Goldberg, "Did it come yet? Did it come yet?" *But how could I write a letter now?* Liba asked herself. *What could I possibly say? That the hotel was in such bad shape that the government wanted to tear it down? That my parents are both very upset and worried and they don't know what to do next? That the people who work at the hotel are the nicest people you could ever hope to meet, and they, too, will have nowhere to go if the hotel is destroyed? No, I cannot write such a letter.*

Liba stopped for a moment to tighten the ribbon at the bottom of her left braid. She loosened her grip on the penny and it fell from her grasp. To her horror, it dropped to the ground and rolled away. She chased after it, desperately hoping it would not roll too far. The small copper-colored piece soon came to rest behind a wooden wagon wheel.

Still clutching her tatty's letter in her right hand, Liba approached the wagon. She noticed two men were sitting beside each other inside. Not wanting them to notice her, she bent down and stuck her hand out under the wagon. The men were talking, and Liba could hear a few

"Miller," Liba hears the men say.
Why are these men discussing my family?

words. *Are they talking English or Afrikaans?* she wondered.

"*Klienten,*" one of the men said; the other one said, "*ide'eh*" and "*ryk.*" *These words sound just like Yiddish,* Liba thought. *These are the words for customers, idea and rich. They must be speaking Afrikaans.* She then heard a few words that she would have understood in any language: "Miller" and "Fifteen Albert Street." *That's our last name! That's the address of Uncle Binam's hotel. Why would these men be discussing my family, and the hotel?*

Liba accidentally pushed the penny even farther away; she had to creep under the wagon to reach it. She heard a few more words, "*genug*" and "*gelt*" — "enough" and "money." Finally, with the tip of her index finger, she managed to reach the penny and drag it toward her. Careful not to bump her head, she crawled out from under the wagon. Holding the penny even tighter than before, she brushed herself off and quickly headed to the post office.

Once inside the building, Liba purchased a stamp; Mr. Glick had been right, it cost one penny. Liba paid and then watched as the woman pasted the stamp on the upper-right-hand corner of the envelope, and put the envelope into a nearby burlap bag. Liba thanked the woman and left the building. She felt very relieved; the letter was now on its way to Mr. Minty's office in Cape Town.

It was only as she began to walk home that Liba thought about what she had overheard a few minutes earlier. She wondered if those men had said all those things, or if she had simply misheard them. Maybe she had made a mistake? Yom Tov had told them that *some* words in Afrikaans were similar to Yiddish, not *all* words. Maybe some of these words meant something totally different in Afrikaans. Or maybe she had imagined hearing these words, because they were some of the very words that were on her mind a lot right now. She wasn't sure.

Chapter Twelve

Liba and her brothers were sitting on an old blanket on the small piece of land at the back of the hotel. Liba was at the front, in the "driver's seat," and the boys were lined up behind her in a row. They were playing "flying blanket," a game Liba had made up years ago. The boys took turns thinking up imaginary places, and Liba "flew" them there.

Liba didn't really feel like playing today. She had only agreed because she knew how much it helped her mama and tatty when she kept her brothers busy. Liba knew that her parents were very worried about the hotel, even though they were trying to act as if everything was fine. She was worried, too. She still felt confused about the conversation she had overheard a few days ago near the post office. She kept asking herself if she had really heard what she had thought she heard, and if she had understood it correctly. If so, what did it mean? She hadn't told her parents about it. After all, she reasoned, they had so much to worry about, she didn't want to make them more upset.

"It's your turn to choose," she said to Hershel.

"I want to go to motorcar land," he suggested.

"What's motorcar land?" asked Chaim.

"It's a land where everyone has a motorcar, even the mamas and the children. No one has to walk anywhere, ever. Whenever you want to go somewhere, you just get in a motorcar and drive yourself there."

Peretz laughed. "That's impossible. Tatty says motorcars are enormously expensive. Only a few very wealthy people can afford to buy them."

"I know it could never happen. This is pretend, remember?" explained Hershel. "Now listen. In motorcar land, there are these special smooth roads. No horses and buggies or carts or wagons are allowed here, or wheelbarrows, either. You can drive really, really fast, and go to lots and lots of nearby towns in only a few minutes."

"So people never walk anywhere again?" Chaim asked, trying to get this clear in his mind. "They never need shoes? They just —"

All of a sudden, Liba heard a familiar noise

coming from the street. She jumped up and said, "*Shh*, Chaim! I think I hear a horse and wagon. Maybe the mailman is here."

The boys scrambled to their feet and followed her to the front of the hotel. They were just in time to see a man in a dark navy uniform get out of a wagon. In his hand he held an envelope.

Liba hurried toward him. "Please! May I help you?" she asked eagerly.

"Yes. I have a letter addressed to Mr. Itzig Miller."

"I am his daughter, Liba Miller."

The man handed her the envelope.

"Thank you, thank you very much," she said.

The man nodded, returned to his wagon and was soon gone.

Liba quickly read the return address. "This is the letter Mama and Tatty have been waiting for, the one from Mr. Minty's office in Cape Town," she told her brothers. "I have to give it to them right away."

"That's all right, Liba. We'll play hide and seek while you're gone," said Chaim.

Liba barely heard what Chaim said. She was already on her way into the hotel. "Mama, Tatty, where are you?" she called as she ran inside.

"Over here, near the front window," said Sorel. She was hanging the curtains she had mended and washed yesterday and Itzig was helping her.

"The letter came from Mr. Minty. Just now," Liba said, as she hurried toward her parents.

Itzig dropped the curtain hooks he had been holding. They clanged noisily to the floor.

"You see, right here, it says 'Ministry of Public Works.'" Liba pointed to the upper-left-hand corner of the envelope.

"I'll ask Yom Tov to translate," said Itzig. He hurried to the front desk. After a predictable wait of a few minutes, Yom Tov appeared, apologizing for the delay. "I am sorry. I was in the middle of something."

"The letter has arrived — we need your help," said Itzig, his voice loud with excitement.

"Of course, of course," said Yom Tov.

Sorel handed him the envelope. Yom Tov quickly ripped it open and pulled out the letter. Not wanting to take the time to unfold it, he simply shook it out so that it unfolded on its own, like a paper fan. His bright green eyes

Yom Tov quickly rips open the envelope
and pulls out the letter.

excitedly scanned the words, but soon grew dull with disappointment.

"*Nu? Nu?*" asked Itzig. "Good news?"

Yom Tov took a deep breath. "Itzig, no. I am sorry. It is not good news."

"What does it say?" asked Sorel.

"It says that although they understand your situation and they sympathize, the department is unable to offer any extensions or make any changes at the present time."

"And?" asked Sorel.

"That is all."

"All?" asked Itzig.

"Yes, I am afraid so. That is all."

Liba muffled a cry. "So, what … what do we do now, Tatty?"

"I don't know," her tatty replied slowly.

Yom Tov offered quietly, "I'll go find Ziesel and Wolf. Maybe they'll know what to do."

"Yes …," Itzig said in a low voice, sounding unconvinced. "Maybe they will."

Chapter Thirteen

"What should we do next?" Mr. Glick repeated Itzig's question, as he awkwardly adjusted the left strap of his overalls. "I am terribly sorry, but I do not know what to do next. What I mean is that I know exactly what to do next, here, in the hotel — the broken headboard in room seven needs to be fixed — but I do not know what to do next, to help. Believe me, if I did, I would certainly be doing it right now, at this very minute. But then again, if I were doing it right now, it wouldn't be what I was doing next, would it? It would be what I was doing now."

Itzig turned to Mrs. Glick. "Do *you* have any suggestions?" he asked wearily.

Mrs. Glick was quiet; she seemed to be thinking something over. "Well, I know of one man in Oudtshoorn who might be able to help us."

"What is his name?"

"Mr. Russell Bartlett."

"Who?" asked Mr. Glick and Yom Tov at the same time.

"Don't you remember? Russell Bartlett. He stayed here many times. He always took room four, at the back, the room with the view of the blue gum trees. His family owned a hat factory in Leeds, England, I believe, and he would visit Oudtshoorn once a year to buy ostrich feathers. I remember he loved my potato kugel. He said it was the best he had ever tasted. Of course, it was the only potato kugel he had ever tasted, but he was very fond of it just the same."

"Oh, yes, I remember him now. Tall, balding fellow, always carried a walking stick," said Yom Tov.

Itzig was having trouble understanding how this information was useful. "How might this man possibly be able to help?" he asked.

"I saw him a few weeks ago, on Queen Street. It seems he is now living in Oudtshoorn. He told me he liked the town so much he decided to stay."

"So he's in the ostrich business, then?" asked Yom Tov.

"No, he is a lawyer. He works from his home.

Maybe if I went to see him and explained the situation, he might give us some advice."

Itzig sighed. "Mrs. Glick, this is a good suggestion. But unfortunately, I don't have any money to pay a lawyer."

"Don't worry about that. I have an idea. Now, if you'll excuse me, I will return to the kitchen. This is urgent."

"What is so urgent?" Sorel asked.

"If I work quickly, I believe I can make one dozen potato kugels for Mr. Bartlett by this evening. What do you think, Itzig?"

"Pay the lawyer with potato kugel?" Itzig asked. He sighed a second time and then threw his hands up in the air. "All right. At this point, I guess it can't hurt."

"Come along, Liba," said Sorel. "Our help is needed in the kitchen."

Sorel was grating onions, Liba was peeling potatoes and Mrs. Glick was measuring the oil. A delicious smell filled the kitchen; the first batch of potato kugels was baking in the oven.

Liba's knife went around and around the

potato, the peel falling to the worn wooden floor at her feet. Her thoughts went around and around, too, and after half an hour or so, she decided to tell her mama about the conversation she had overheard the other day.

"Mama," she said hesitantly, "I need to tell you about something. Something important."

Her mama looked up, concern in her clear blue eyes. "What is it, Liba'le?"

Liba put down the potato. Trying to remember as many details as possible, she told her mama all about what had happened when she went to mail the letter. When she was finished, she asked, "Do you think Mrs. Glick should mention this when she visits the lawyer tomorrow?"

"No, my dear. Mrs. Glick will tell him only what we know for certain, what we were told by Mr. Minty. She cannot tell him about a conversation that you may or may not have heard."

"Mama, I am pretty sure I heard those words: 'Idea.' 'Money.' 'Rich.' 'Customers.'"

"My dear," said her mama softly, "you said the men appeared to be speaking Afrikaans. You don't know this language. You easily could have mixed up a few Afrikaans words with a few

Liba's mama looks up, concern in her clear blue eyes. "What is it, Liba'le?"

similar-sounding words in Yiddish, words that mean something entirely different."

"But what about the words 'Miller' and 'Fifteen Albert Street'? They can't mean anything other than what we understand them to mean."

"Liba, you told me that you were crouching underneath a wagon. How clearly could you have heard what was being said?"

"I guess you're right," said Liba. She went back to peeling her potato, but then something else suddenly occurred to her.

"Mama, one more thing."

"Yes?"

"I didn't think anything of it at the time, but do you remember the first day in Oudtshoorn, when Mrs. Glick took us for that long walk on *Der Yiddishe Gass*?"

"Yes, I do."

"When we came back, the boys ran into the house to tell you about everything they had seen, but I stopped for a minute to buckle my shoe. I saw a man run from the back of the hotel."

"You saw a man run from the back of the hotel?"

"Yes. At least, I think I saw him. Maybe he

was looking at the hotel, maybe he was planning to do something to it, and maybe — just maybe — he was one of the men I overheard talking in the wagon."

Her mama put down the onion she was grating and laid a gentle hand on Liba's shoulder.

"Liba," she said, looking directly at her, "your tatty and I have always felt that Hashem blessed you with a special gift — a wonderful imagination. When you were a little girl, you made up so many stories ... Do you remember? They were about all sorts of things — mysterious strangers, princesses in palaces, evil villains and friendly giants. You and Bayla kept yourselves occupied for hours, acting out these stories. When you got older, you thought up so many exciting games and activities for Peretz and Hershel and Chaim — like "flying blanket." You always managed to keep your brothers busy and happy. It was a tremendous help to me."

"Thank you, Mama."

"But right now, in this situation, your imagination is not helpful."

"What do you mean?"

"I know you are worried about what is going

to happen — all of us are — but you are letting your imagination get the better of you. Liba, think logically for a minute. Your tatty and I came here because Uncle Binam left us the hotel in his will, as a gift. We hoped that with Hashem's help, we might be able to make a better life here. But why would anyone who already lives here — a South African — possibly want this hotel? You live here, and you know that it is in very bad shape — the furniture is old and battered, the floorboards are loose and the windows are cracked. It requires a tremendous amount of repair."

Her mama leaned over and gave Liba a light kiss on the top of her head. "Please, dear, try not to think about this anymore. Don't upset yourself."

"All right, Mama, I will try."

Her mama returned to the onions and the grater. "We must get back to work. We have a lot to do."

Chapter Fourteen

The next morning, Liba helped Mrs. Glick carry the potato kugels to Mr. Bartlett's house. She had intended to go straight home as soon as she dropped them off, but as she turned to leave, Mr. Bartlett's wife put a light hand on her arm and said, "You must have a cool drink before you head back. It is becoming quite hot outside." She showed Liba into the parlor. "Please, take a seat. I will be back in one minute," she said.

Liba sat down on a high-backed red velvet sofa. She looked around the room, admiring the thick rug in the middle of the polished wooden floor, the collection of pretty plates and tea cups displayed in the china cabinet and the fine tapestry that hung on the far wall. A delicate chandelier hung directly above a long wooden table. Liba counted ten chairs on either side. *Imagine eating at such a long table*, she thought. *No one's elbows or hands*

would bump into anyone else's; everyone would have enough room.

Mrs. Bartlett returned, carrying a glass of water on a small silver tray. She handed the glass to Liba and sat down in a nearby chair. "You don't look familiar. I don't believe I have seen you in town. Have you just arrived?"

"Yes, my family and I have been here a little over two weeks."

"Your English is excellent, I must say."

"Thank you."

"Where are you living, if you don't mind my asking?"

"On Albert Street." Liba said a quiet *brachah* to herself and took a quick sip of water.

"Oh, yes, Albert Street. It is in a lovely part of town, though I haven't been there in a long time. Many years ago I stayed at Miller's Hotel. Have they started to tear it down?"

Liba wasn't sure if she understood the question. What did Mrs. Bartlett mean, "Have they started to tear it down?" Was she simply making conversation, or had she somehow heard about Mr. Minty's visit?

"No," Liba replied.

"They haven't started building the emporium yet?"

"Emp … emp… *emporium*?" Liba shook her head. She didn't know the word.

"John Olive's Ostrich Emporium. It is a brilliant idea. It is surprising that no one thought of it before. It will be a huge store that sells everything connected to ostriches. One half of the emporium will cater to the ostrich farmers. It will have incubators for the baby ostriches and wood to build pens for the older ostriches, and ostrich feed — alfalfa, soy and corn. The other half of the store will have products for everyone else — ostrich meat and ostrich leather and, of course, thousands of ostrich feathers."

Trying to keep her voice steady, Liba asked, "Where did you say they are building this big store?"

"On the property belonging to Miller's Hotel. My husband and I were at Olive's Ostrich Farm a few weeks ago, buying feathers to ship to England. My husband asked how business was, and Mr. Olive said it was better than ever — that his plans for the emporium were going well and they were set to start building very soon. It had taken him a long time and a lot of money, he said, but he had finally been able to get his hands on the perfect spot."

Liba sat up with a jolt, sloshing the water in her glass. *This Mr. Olive must be the man I overheard in the wagon, the day I went to the post office! He must have been telling the other man about building this new store, talking about the customers he would have and all the money he would make!*

"Mrs. Bartlett, may I ask you a question?"

"Yes, of course."

"Does Mr. Olive speak Afrikaans?"

"I would think so. He is originally from England, just like my husband and I, but he has lived in Oudtshoorn for years. He must have learned the language by now."

Liba jumped to her feet. The water spilled out of her glass and onto the front of her dress.

"Excuse me, Mrs. Bartlett, I am terribly sorry."

"Is something wrong?"

"No, not at all. I mean, yes, there is. What I mean to say is ... " Liba suddenly forgot how to speak English properly. "Must goes. Mama be waiting. Thanks you nicely."

Liba jumps to her feet. "Excuse me, Mrs. Bartlett, I am terribly sorry."

Liba thrust the glass into the startled woman's hands and bolted from the parlor. She dashed through the hall and out the front door. Her long blond braids swinging wildly behind her, she ran the entire way back to Miller's Hotel.

* * *

"Just a minute. I am in the middle of something," a familiar voice called.

In the middle of something, again? Why is Yom Tov always 'in the middle of something'? The middle of what, exactly? Liba thought as she stood at the front desk, drumming her fingers on the counter with impatience.

She had to speak with Yom Tov immediately, she just had to. She remembered what he had said right after Mr. Minty had been at the hotel. His exact words were, "The man offered to buy the hotel, but Binam refused. The man said, 'Miller, you're a fool. You will never get a better offer. Never.'"

Liba was absolutely certain this man was Mr. Olive, the man Mrs. Bartlett had just told her about. Mr. Olive wanted to buy the hotel from Uncle Binam because he wanted to build his emporium on the property.

Where is Yom Tov? Why is he always in the middle of something? What exactly is he doing back there? I can't stand here and wait for hours, I just can't ...

Liba couldn't wait any longer. She knew it wasn't right, but she went behind the counter and pushed open the door on the right side, the door Yom Tov always came out of. She immediately found herself in a small room. Yom Tov was standing directly under a small oil lamp, his tall frame hunched over a tiny table. He was holding a few pieces of metal in his hands.

Yom Tov looked up, startled. "What are you doing here?" he asked as he moved his small oval-shaped glasses higher up on the bridge of his nose.

Liba took a quick look around. The walls were covered with pictures, many pictures of ... teeth? Was she imagining this? She hoped not; her mama had warned her yesterday about letting her imagination get the better of her.

"What are *you* doing here?" Liba asked.

"I am working. This is my workroom."

"Are you a dentist?"

"No, not at all. I am an inventor."

Liba noticed that Yom Tov blushed deeply as he said this; his face turned almost the same shade of red as his hair. "You invent things? Why?"

"Well," Yom Tov began, still blushing, "as you know, soon after the Royal Crown opened, we began to lose customers. I was worried that Binam would not be able to keep Miller's Hotel running. I thought that if I could invent something very important, something very useful, I could sell the invention for a lot of money. I could then use this money to help keep the hotel open. I have been working on my invention for years. I am getting really close, but it is not quite ready yet."

"What does this have to do with teeth?" asked Liba, pointing to the pictures on the wall.

"My invention is called the 'clothes-close.' It is meant to replace all the different devices people use to fasten their clothing — buttons, snaps, laces, hooks and eyes. The clothes-close would join two sides of a garment together — like a jacket, for instance — and keep them shut, properly and securely. Wouldn't that be tremendously helpful?"

The conversation was so odd, yet so interesting, that Liba found herself briefly forgetting the reason she had wanted to speak to Yom Tov in the first place.

"I guess so. But what does that have to do with teeth?" Liba asked.

"Think about it. Your upper teeth and lower teeth work together perfectly. They line up in two rows and they lock together, allowing you to keep things either inside or outside of your mouth. The clothes-close would do the same. A chain made up of a row of metal pieces — 'teeth,' if you will — would be sewn into either side of a piece of fabric. These teeth would somehow be drawn together, line up and lock. And so, I study teeth to try to figure out exactly how this works. My favorite teeth to study are crocodile teeth. They are the biggest."

"Oh, that is why you like visiting Mr. Kruger's crocodile farm. That is why you had a small notebook with you and you drew that sketch when you took us there."

"Yes, exactly. The sketch I drew that day is hanging right over there." Yom Tov pointed to the far side of the room.

"I see," said Liba.

"While you are here, may I ask you a question about my invention?" Yom Tov asked.

"Certainly."

"What do you think about the name, 'the clothes-close'?"

"Mmm." Liba thought this over as she fiddled with the end of her left braid. "It certainly is easy to remember, but what about something a bit more ... more fun-sounding?"

"Like what?"

"Well, what sort of sound do you think the clothes-close would make?"

"I haven't ever thought about it. Maybe like a zzziizzziiizppp, the sound of all the metal teeth working together and locking into place," said Yom Tov.

"How about calling it 'the zzzzippper'?"*

"That's not a bad idea. I'll think it over. Thank you. It was worth having you barge into my workroom after all."

Liba was suddenly brought back to the reason of her unexpected visit. "Oh, yes, I am terribly

* The modern-day zipper was invented in 1913 by a Swedish-born Canadian engineer named Gideon Sundback.

sorry. It is just that I have a question for you, a very important question, and I couldn't wait. I know it was very rude of me."

"There was no harm done. Now, tell me, what is the question?"

"You mentioned that a few years ago, a man wanted to buy the hotel from Uncle Binam, but that Uncle Binam refused. You said you could not remember his name."

"Yes, that it correct. It was maybe five years ago, right after I had started working on the clothes-close."

"Is it possible that his name was John Olive?"

"Yes! It was! Exactly! Mr. John Olive. Medium build, bushy mustache. Why?"

"Oh, no! I must speak with Mama and Tatty immediately. Thank you! Thank you very much! I will explain everything later."

Liba darted out of the workroom, leaving behind a very confused Yom Tov.

Chapter Fifteen

"Please, Liba, slow down," said Sorel as she handed a hammer to Itzig. "We can't understand what you are saying when you talk so quickly."

Liba took a deep breath and began again. "After Mrs. Glick and I delivered the potato kugels to Mr. Bartlett, his wife told me to sit down in her parlor and have a rest, and a drink. She brought me a glass of water and she started to talk to me, to ask me questions. When I told her where we live, she said that a man named John Olive, an ostrich farmer who lives in Oudtshoorn, is planning on building a giant store right here, on this very property. He told her so himself. I immediately remembered that Yom Tov had told us that a man wanted to buy the hotel a few years ago. I ran all the way home and asked Yom Tov if the man's name was John Olive. And it was! It was! Mama, the man I heard at the post office must have been this

John Olive. Mrs. Bartlett says he most certainly speaks Afrikaans. So, you see, I really did hear all those words. It wasn't my imagination."

Her tatty banged another nail into the bookcase that was lying on its side. "Liba," he said, as he put down his hammer, "this conversation with Mrs. Bartlett took place in English, am I correct?"

"Yes, Tatty, it did. I know what you are thinking — that maybe I misunderstood what she said. But you know that ever since we were on the ship, I have been working very hard to learn English. I always ask Mrs. Glick to speak to me in English and to give me books to read in English. Mrs. Bartlett said I spoke it very well. I really think I understood what she was saying."

"Sorel, on the count of three, lift the right side of the bookcase," instructed her tatty, as he took hold of the left side. "One, two, three," he said. Liba watched as her parents worked together to lift it to a standing position.

Itzig took a close look at his handiwork. "Not bad, not bad at all," he said, an expression of satisfaction on his face.

"Yes, Itzig. Fine work," said Sorel.

"Mama! Tatty! Are you listening?"

"Yes, dear, we are," said her mama. "Liba, I think I know what happened."

"You do?"

"Yes. The woman told you that this conversation took place at an ostrich farm. She obviously misheard what was being said. This Mr. Olive must have said that he was going to build a store on Albert Street, *near* Miller's Hotel, not *on* Miller's Hotel. Mrs. Glick told me that those big birds can be terribly loud. They make a deep, throaty noise, something like, 'whoo, whoooo, whoooo.'"

"Whoo, whooo, whoooo, Mama?"

"Yes, according to Mrs. Glick, that is the sound they make when they are frightened."

In spite of herself, Liba started to laugh. "You'd make a very funny ostrich, Mama."

"Why, thank you, dear," said her mama with a smile, enjoying the sound of her daughter's laughter.

"Mama, do you really think Mrs. Bartlett misheard? She sounded so very sure of herself."

"Yes, dear, I really do think so."

"Tatty, do you think so, too?"

"Yes, I think Mama is absolutely right."

"But … but … but … don't you think it is strange that the man who is going to build that big store is the same man who tried to buy the hotel years ago from Uncle Binam?"

"Not at all," said her tatty. "It could very well be the same person. As I am sure you remember, back home in Kelm I worked in a lumberyard. The owner of the yard always wanted to expand but no one would sell him the surrounding land. Every few years, he would approach a few of the neighbors and ask if they had changed their minds, but they always refused. If one had ever agreed, he would have been very happy to buy their land — and for a high price, too, I am willing to guess. This is most probably the same situation. Over the past few years, Mr. Olive has no doubt approached a number of people on Albert Street and asked if he could buy their property. Eventually, someone agreed and now he is able to build his new store. This sort of thing happens all the time. There is nothing strange about it at all."

"I guess so, Mama and Tatty," said Liba. She wanted to believe that her parents were right, but for some reason, she was not entirely convinced.

* ✻ *

As she ladled the cabbage borscht out of an enormous soup pot, Mrs. Glick began to describe what had happened earlier that day at Mr. Bartlett's office. It was clear to everyone seated at the dinner table that she was very upset. Instead of her usual cheerful voice, she spoke in hushed tones, barely lifting her eyes to meet anyone's gaze.

Mrs. Glick said that after tasting the potato kugel and pronouncing it delicious — the best he had ever tasted — Mr. Bartlett ushered her into his office. Mrs. Glick was very pleased; it had seemed the meeting was off to a good start. As she recounted Mr. Minty's visit to the hotel and told him everything the official had said, Mr. Bartlett jotted down a few notes on a sheet of paper. After about five minutes or so, he gently interrupted her. "Please, Mrs. Glick, I believe I have heard enough," he said. He then told her that he would like to help, but it would take many hours to look into the matter. Even though he really enjoyed her potato kugel, he simply did not have the time.

Mrs. Glick had fought hard to hold back her

tears. She thanked Mr. Bartlett and promptly left his office. Mrs. Bartlett had then approached her in the front hall and asked her a number of unusual questions: Was Liba feeling all right? Did she perhaps have a touch of sunstroke? Was she making sure to drink enough in this hot weather? So anxious was she to leave that Mrs. Glick didn't stop to ask the woman the reason for her sudden interest in the state of Liba's health. She simply mumbled a quick good-bye and hurried out of the house.

"If only I had taken him a few jars of my mushroom-barley soup," Mrs. Glick said sadly. "Everyone loves my mushroom-barley soup. It all would have been different." Mrs. Glick then put the ladle down directly on the table, not noticing that a little bit of soup was still inside. It spilled out and began to stain the tablecloth a dark red.

"Mrs. Glick, please do not blame yourself. This had nothing to do with your food. Mr. Bartlett is simply too busy to help us," said Itzig.

"You don't understand. This soup works wonders. Once, a *smous* who stayed with us for a few days somehow lost his bag full of the goods

"If only I had taken him a few jars of my mushroom-barley soup," says Mrs. Glick.

he had hoped to sell. He was very upset. He ate one bowl of my mushroom-barley soup and he cheered up immediately. Another time a young girl stayed here overnight on her way to visit her grandparents in Calitzdorp. Her parents were not with her, and she was very homesick. One bowl of my soup, and the child was smiling and laughing the entire evening."

Mrs. Glick picked up the ladle and continued serving the cabbage borscht.

Throughout the rest of the meal, Mr. Glick tried his best to cheer up his wife. He described, in great detail, all the delicious food she had cooked and baked since 1895, the year they both had started working at Miller's Hotel. He spent over ten minutes talking about the time in August 1903 when she had prepared a fancy, five-course Shabbos dinner for a traveling rabbi, his wife and six children — with only one hour's notice. It did not help; Mrs. Glick remained unhappy.

Liba was not feeling particularly cheerful, either. She continued to think about the events of the past few weeks — the man dashing from the back of the hotel, Mr. Minty's visit and his terrible announcement, the strange conversation between those two men in the wagon, Mr. Olive's plan to start building an emporium on Albert Street, and learning from Yom Tov that Mr. Olive was the man who had once tried to buy the hotel from Uncle Binam. As much as she wanted to believe her parents' explanations, Liba had the feeling that something else, something more, was behind all this.

If only Bayla were here, Liba thought as she stirred a piece of cabbage in her bowl. *I could tell her everything, just like I used to back home in Kelm, and we would sit and discuss it for hours. Even if Bayla couldn't help me figure it out, she would make me laugh with one of her well-timed jokes, or by wiggling her ears or doing a handstand. And that would be helpful, too.*

Chapter Sixteen

Later that night, Liba took her nightgown out of the wobbly little chest of drawers in her room. She was preparing to go to sleep. As she unfolded the nightgown, a button came loose and fell off in her hand. Liba frowned. She would have to sew the button back on tomorrow, and she did not like to sew.

A thought suddenly occurred to her. *If only this nightgown had Yom Tov's invention, the clothes-close. I would never have to sew another button on it again!* Liba imagined herself wearing a brand new pink cotton nightgown with long full sleeves and delicate ruffles at the neckline and the wrists. Using two sets of teeth that worked together, just as Yom Tov had described, it would close easily at the top and stay closed.

Liba untied the two small ribbons that kept her braids in place and loosened her hair. She took her hairbrush out of the top drawer of the chest and continued to think about the clothes-close. Two sides working together — it was a brilliant idea, really. She hoped Yom Tov would be able to make it work.

"Working together, working together," she said to herself as she brushed out her long hair. *What did this remind me of? Mama and Tatty had worked together earlier today to fix that bookcase. They had done an excellent job, and it looked as good as new. But somewhere else, some other people had been working together. Who?*

Liba suddenly thought of it — Mr. Minty and Mr. Olive. Could they possibly be working together? Could these two men somehow be connected? It seemed unlikely. One man was an important government official, with his own car and driver, who worked all the way over in Cape Town; the other man was a local ostrich farmer here in Oudtshoorn, planning on opening a store. And yet, something about the timing of their plans was strangely coincidental. A few weeks ago, Mr. Minty had shown up and told everyone that the hotel had to be closed by the end of the January. According to what Mrs.

Bartlett had told Liba earlier today, the end of January was when Mr. Olive wanted to start building his emporium.

It didn't seem possible, but somehow, in some way, it made perfect sense to her. The two men were connected; they were working together. Liba just had to figure out how.

* * *

"What in the world are you doing?" Liba cried, nearly slipping on a small puddle of water in the lobby.

"We're playing pirates," Chaim announced proudly.

"Pirates?" she asked. "What does that have to do with this water all over the floor?"

"Liba," said Chaim, slowly and carefully, as if he were explaining something complicated to someone much younger than himself, "pirates live on ships, on the open sea. We poured some water on the floor, just a tiny bit, to make it seem more real."

"And look at our pirate hats," said Hershel, pointing to his head.

Liba now noticed that all three of her brothers

were wearing hats that seemed to have been made from folded up pieces of newspaper.

"Where did you get these?" she asked. Without waiting for an answer, she added quickly, "I know. Yom Tov made these for you, didn't he?"

"Yes, he did. How did you guess?" asked Peretz.

"I know he likes to make things. Did you happen to tell Yom Tov that you were planning to pour water all over the floor in the lobby?"

"Not all over the floor, Liba. A tiny bit, just a tiny bit," repeated Chaim.

"Did you tell him?" Liba asked, more sternly this time.

"Liba, don't be silly. He didn't want to know all the details. He wasn't interested in playing with us. He saw us running around the lobby and he asked what we were doing. When we told him we were pretending to be pirates, he said he would make us special pirate hats. Aren't they great?"

Liba ignored Hershel's question. "Listen to me. If Mama and Tatty walk into the lobby this morning and see all this water on the floor, or slip, *chas v'shalom*, just like I almost did, they are going to be very, very upset. The three of you need to clean this up right away. Go into the kitchen and ask Mrs. Glick to borrow her mop."

"Liba, that's no fun. No fun at all. Why are you so grumpy all of a sudden?" asked Hershel.

"I'm not grumpy," Liba answered. She then realized that she did indeed sound a little grumpy. "All right," she said, her voice softer. "Here's an idea. When you ask Mrs. Glick for her mop, also ask her — very politely, mind you — if you might also borrow a rolling pin."

"A rolling pin? What for? Pirates don't make cookies, they steal treasures. You know that, Liba," said Chaim.

"Listen. A rolling pin is long and narrow, the same shape as a telescope. Once you finish mopping the floor, you can use the rolling pin to pretend you are looking out to sea."

The boys looked at each other again. "What do you think, Peretz?" asked Hershel.

"Aye-aye, matey!"

Hershel and Peretz dashed out of the lobby and headed toward the kitchen.

"Mates, mates, wait for me," cried Chaim, as he ran after them.

Chaim's hat fell from his head, narrowly missing a small puddle. He didn't stop; he was in a hurry to catch up to his older brothers. Liba knew he would be upset if he came back to find that his hat was ruined, so she picked it up from the floor.

As she held it in her hands, Liba took a closer look at the way it was made. It seemed that Yom Tov had taken one piece of newspaper and folded it in half. Then he had folded the tops down on either side to make triangles, and then he had folded the bottom flap up on one side, and then the other. *This is very simple, but very clever,* she thought. *It would be perfect for Purim.* A word at the bottom of the hat suddenly caught her eye. Was she reading this correctly or was she simply imagining it because it was a word that was now on her mind almost all the time? She read each letter out loud, slowly, just to be sure: *M-I-N-T-Y*. Then she said the word out loud, too: Minty.

Forgetting that it belonged to Chaim and that he certainly was expecting to play with it again in a few minutes, Liba unfolded the hat. It now was a piece of newspaper again. She gasped.

Liba takes a closer look
at Chaim's pirate hat.

There it was, in big black letters across the front page of yesterday's paper. The headline read: **Lionel Minty Arrested in Cape Town**.

Chapter Seventeen

Her hands trembling, Liba slowly read:

January 17, 1911 — Cape Town, Union of South Africa

Mr. Lionel Minty, 53, assistant to the chief inspector, National Buildings Regulations and Building Standards, the Ministry of Public Works, was arrested late Tuesday afternoon on three charges of bribery. A six-week-long investigation revealed that since being appointed to his present position three months ago, Minty, in exchange for large sums of money, pronounced various buildings in violation of the ministry's standards, when in fact there were no such violations. When questioned about his motives, Minty simply replied, "I wanted more." It is unclear at the present time if Minty had wanted more of an important role in the Union of South Africa's new government, or if he had simply wanted more money. The investigation continues. Those close to the investigation say that more charges are likely.

Just to make sure she correctly understood what she was reading, Liba forced herself to read it a second time, even more slowly.

This explains everything! Unable to buy the property directly from Uncle Binam, Mr. Olive had given Mr. Minty money — a lot of money — to come to Oudtshoorn and tell Tatty that the government had ordered that Miller's Hotel be closed. Just as I had suspected, the men had been working together!

"Mama, Tatty, everyone! Quick! Come to the lobby immediately — please — it's urgent!" Liba yelled.

Mr. Glick came running, a look of bewilderment on his face and a screwdriver in his hand. Mrs. Glick soon followed, holding a rolling pin and trailed by Liba's three little brothers. Yom Tov emerged from his workroom a few minutes later.

"Mama! Tatty! You have to hear this! Where are you?" Liba yelled even louder this time.

Her parents hurried into the lobby, looking

alarmed. "We were in room ten, at the very end of the hall. Why are you yelling? Tell me, what is wrong?" her mama demanded.

"Look!" Liba said, as she thrust the newspaper into her mama's hands.

"Liba, that was my hat!" cried Chaim.

"I'm sorry. There was something I had to read. I'll make you another one, very soon."

"With the same big folds at the sides?"

"Please, Chaim, not now."

"Exactly the same, with the big folds at the sides?" he asked again.

"Yes, yes, fine. Later, not now."

Her mama handed the newspaper back to Liba. "I am sorry, I can't read this. It's in English. Tatty can't read it, either."

"Oh, of course, I forgot. Mr. Glick, please, could you read it?" asked Liba.

Mr. Glick put his screwdriver into the bib pocket of his overalls and took hold of the paper in his small plump hands. He read for a few seconds and then he said, "Sorel, Itzig, this is shocking news. No, let me correct myself. This is very shocking news. I would even say, extremely shocking news. Yes, extremely shocking, extremely. That is, of course, if you are the sort of person who is usually shocked by reading articles in the newspaper. I would say, however, that in this particular instance, even people who are not usually shocked would find this shocking. Perhaps they would find it merely shocking, or simply very shocking, but yes, there is a chance that they might find it extremely shocking, too."

"Wolf, please, let me have that," said Mrs. Glick, taking the newspaper away from her husband. With Yom Tov looking over her shoulder, she began to read. Every few seconds or so she would say a word out loud. "Minty… arrested… bribes… more…"

"You see, it all makes sense now," said Liba, her voice loud with excitement. "Mr. Minty came here and told us the hotel was in violation of all sorts of codes. That way, he would have an excuse to force us to leave and then he would tear down the building. But really, although the hotel is old and in need of repair, none of what he said was true. Mr. Olive paid Mr. Minty to do this because Mr. Olive wanted to build his ostrich emporium on this property."

Everyone waits anxiously as Mrs. Glick begins to read the newspaper article.

Liba looked at her tatty and continued. “Tatty, all you have to do now is write another letter to the government and explain that Mr. Minty came here and that he accepted money from Mr. Olive. Then they will write back and tell us that we can stay here as long as we want.”

Itzig shook his head. “Liba, from what I have been able to understand, Mr. Minty broke the law. He did something very dishonest. But where does it say in the newspaper that he took money from Mr. Olive — that he had anything to do with Mr. Olive at all?”

Liba was astonished. What was her tatty suggesting?

“But, Tatty, it says the investigation is continuing. I am sure it is only a matter of time before the people in charge realize Mr. Minty took bribes in Oudtshoorn, too. That is why all you have to do is write another letter, and then — ”

“Liba, I will not write any such letter,” interrupted Itzig, his tone firm.

“Why, Tatty? Isn’t it possible I am right?”

“Perhaps.”

“But then —”

"Liba, you must understand. We are recent Jewish immigrants, very new to this country. How can I, Itzig Miller, send a letter to the government accusing one of their officials of doing something wrong? What if I am mistaken? This could make Mr. Minty, or someone else, angry. Very angry. It is a risk I am not willing to take." Her tatty gestured around the room, at his family and at the staff of the hotel. "There is too much for all of us to lose, Liba."

"But … but …" Liba was so frustrated that she burst into tears. Her mama rushed to put her arm around Liba's shoulders. "Please, dear, don't upset yourself."

She then turned to her husband and said, "Itzig, I have a suggestion."

"Yes?" he asked.

"Maybe someone should go to Mr. Olive's ostrich farm and speak to him, to ask him a few questions. Not, *chas v'shalom*, to accuse him of doing anything wrong, but just to get the facts straight. In this way, we could find out exactly what his plans are. If he says he is planning to build his store on the property of this hotel, it might be worth trying to find out if he ever had any dealings with Mr. Minty. If he says that he is building his store on a different property, we will know that Mr. Minty's visit here had nothing to do with him."

Itzig thought this over for a moment. "Yes, Sorel, I believe this makes good sense," he said.

"Tatty, maybe you and Mama could go," Liba suggested.

"No, impossible. Our English is not good enough. Besides, if Mr. Olive did indeed bribe Mr. Minty to come here and tell me the hotel has to be torn down, Mr. Olive certainly knows my name."

"Yom Tov?" asked Liba.

The young man shook his head. "I am afraid not. If you remember, I was standing with Binam that day a few years ago when Mr. Olive approached him about buying the hotel. If he remembers me, if he knows that I am connected to the hotel, he will certainly not admit to wanting to build a store here."

"Mrs. Glick?" asked Liba hopefully.

Mrs. Glick sighed loudly. "I would dearly love to help, Liba — you know that I would. But after my upsetting meeting yesterday with Mr.

Bartlett, I am afraid I am simply not up to it. I do hope you understand."

"Of course, Ziesel, we understand," said Sorel kindly.

The only English-speaking adult that Liba had not asked was Mr. Glick. Everyone now turned to look at him.

"Me?" he asked, sounding surprised.

"Ah, um, yes, well, I guess so," said Liba, with little enthusiasm.

"Itzig, if you need me, I will do it," said Mr. Glick.

"Thank you," said Itzig. "Are you able to go today? I want to have this settled once and for all."

"Yes. I can leave now. I believe I know where Mr. Olive's farm is located. I passed it once a number of years ago."

"You're going to the ostrich farm now?" asked Hershel.

"Yes, it seems that I am."

"But we want to go, too. Don't we, Peretz? Don't we, Chaim?"

"Yes, yes, we do, we do!" they cried at the same time.

"We've been looking forward to this for weeks, ever since Mrs. Glick told us about the ostrich feathers. Please, Tatty, please? We'll be very good. We won't bother anyone. We just want to see the ostriches," said Hershel.

Itzig thought this over. "You just want to see the ostriches? You won't get in the way?"

"No, we won't get in the way at all," said Hershel.

"Liba, are you willing to go along, to keep an eye on the boys?" asked her mama.

"Yes, I guess so."

"Wait right here, boys, Liba," said Mr. Glick. "I will be back in no time, no time at all. What I mean, of course, is that it will take *some* time, but that this time will be so small, so insignificant, and I will be back so very soon, so quickly, that you will feel as if no time has passed, no time whatsoever. And then we will be on our way to pay a visit to Mr. Olive."

Itzig and Sorel exchanged brief looks. They hoped this was a good idea.

Chapter Eighteen

Mr. Glick pulled up near a small sign. "Olive's Ostrich Farm" was spelled out in black letters.

"We're here," he announced as he stepped down from his seat. Everyone got out of the wagon. "Boys," Liba reminded her brothers, "you are not to do any talking. Just looking."

"Yes, Liba, we'll remember," said Chaim.

"Let's go," said Mr. Glick, brushing off the dust from his overalls. "The time is now. I mean, the actual time is 2:14 p.m., but this seems to be as good a time as any to meet Mr. Olive."

Mr. Glick led everyone along a narrow dirt path toward a low wooden building. Peretz noticed a small gate attached to its left side. Pointing toward it, he said, "That must be an ostrich pen. Mr. Glick, can we stop for a moment to see the ostriches?"

"Allow me to speak with Mr. Olive first," replied Mr. Glick. "Before we leave, we will take a look at the ostriches. Maybe more than one look, if you and your brothers find it very interesting. Maybe even two or three. Follow me."

They soon reached the building. Mr. Glick knocked loudly on the front door. A man with a big brown mustache quickly appeared. "Hello, sir, how may I help you?" he asked Mr. Glick.

"Hello, sir, to you, too. I am not so much looking for help as I am looking for Mr. Olive. Mr. John Olive. Would you possibly know where I might find him? Not that he is missing, it is just that I myself do not know where he is."

"I am Mr. John Olive. And who might you be?"

"I am Mr. Zev Wolf Glick. As far as I know, I might not be anyone else."

"How may I help you?" asked Mr. Olive.

Peretz, Hershel and Chaim began to grow restless. They had come to the farm because they wanted to see the ostriches, not to stand and listen to Mr. Glick talk to Mr. Olive. They began to kick at the dusty dirt beneath their feet. Peretz unearthed a tiny feather with his right shoe. Only an inch or so in length, it was a light cream color.

"I found an ostrich feather," he whispered to Hershel as he bent down and picked it up. He brushed it off and ran his fingers along its soft, weightless sides. He then leaned toward Chaim and tickled him under his nose. Chaim sneezed.

"I myself have lived on Albert Street for a number of years," Mr. Glick continued.

"Achoo!" Chaim sneezed a second time.

Liba turned to look at him. "*SHH!*" she said.

"Liba, I can't help it. You know that when I sneeze, the more I try to hold it in, the louder it gets," Chaim whispered.

Peretz and Hershel continued to kick at the dirt. Hershel kicked a bit too hard, and a small cloud of dust rose from the ground and blew into their faces.

"*Cough, cough, cough,*" went Hershel.

"*Cough, cough, cough,*" went Peretz.

"*Achoo, achoo,*" went Chaim.

"Boys, *shh*!" said Liba, again.

Mr. Olive seemed to notice the boys for the first time. He looked at them and said, "Ostriches are very sensitive to germs. If you are not well, I ask that you leave my farm immediately."

"The boys are fine. I am sorry," Liba quickly reassured the man.

"*Achoo, achoo,*" went Chaim.

"*Cough, cough, cough,*" went Peretz and Hershel.

A faint hissing sound could now be heard coming from somewhere nearby.

"What is that?" asked Mr. Glick.

"My ostriches. Their hearing is excellent. The racket your children are making is upsetting them."

The hissing grew louder. "*HISS... HISS...*"

"*Achoo, achoo, achoo.*"

"*Cough, cough, cough.*"

"*SHH! SHH! SHH!*"

"*HISS... HISS... HISS...*"

Mr. Glick raised his voice to make sure he was heard over the strange variety of noises. "As I was saying, in recent days — well, just yesterday, to be precise — I heard talk that you are planning to build an emporium, that is, a very large store, to sell all sorts of ostrich products."

"Yes, that's correct," replied Mr. Olive, anxiously looking past Mr. Glick toward his ostrich pen.

A faint, high-pitched screaming began. It quickly grew louder, and then, suddenly, a booming noise was heard. "*Who, whoo, whooo.*"

The boys were so startled that all their sneezing and coughing immediately stopped.

"You've frightened my birds, you naughty children!" Mr. Olive yelled. He began to run toward the pen.

Mr. Glick and the children quickly followed. When they reached the pen, they were astonished by what they saw. Three huge birds, each one over ten feet tall, were running around in circles, flapping their giant wings. Their heavy bodies were covered with layer upon layer of grayish brown feathers, and were supported by incredibly long, thin, featherless legs. Their long narrow necks moved back and forth; their black eyes, set far apart on either side of their tiny, bald heads, were huge with annoyance. "*WHO, WHOO, WHOOO!*" the ostriches boomed, over and over again. The sound reminded Liba of the foghorn used by the crew on the ship that had brought her family to South Africa.

As Mr. Olive bent down to scoop something out of a nearby bucket, Mr. Glick said, "A few people who live on Albert Street want to know exactly what the new address will be, when indeed your new store opens. Would you possibly be willing to give it to me today? No need to write it down, of course. You can just tell me,

"You've frightened my birds, you naughty children!" Mr. Olive yells.

and I will do my best to remember."

Mr. Olive spun around to face Mr. Glick. "Be quiet! I have to calm my birds!" he said. Mr. Olive then pushed open the gate to the pen and stepped in, staying close to the side. "Millicent, Harriet, Gertrude," he called in a soft singsong, as he held out his hand. "There is nothing to get excited about. Come here. Daddy has a nice snack."

Liba and her brothers looked at each other, confused. *Millicent? Harriet? Gertrude? Daddy?*

The ostriches were clearly in no mood for a nice snack. Millicent — or was it Harriet? Or Gertrude? — ran toward Mr. Olive and shot one of her long skinny legs toward him, her huge toenail narrowly missing his left arm. "*AAHH!*" he shouted in alarm. He threw the feed up in the air as if it were confetti, dashed out of the pen and slammed the gate closed behind him.

"You see what you've done, with all your sneezing and your coughing?" he shouted at the boys. "And you with your constant shushing?" he yelled at Liba. "My birds are in a complete state of nervous anxiety. It will take hours for them to calm down. Hours!"

Turning to Mr. Glick, he demanded, "And you,

with all your long-winded comments and questions. What do you want? The address of the emporium? You came all the way out here to my farm just to ask me this? You couldn't have waited to see for yourself, when it opened? Fine. It will be built on 15 Albert Street, on the property of that old, run-down, poor excuse for a hotel, just as soon as Miller's family gets out of there."

"Did you say '*on* 15 Albert Street, *on* the property of that old, run-down, poor excuse for a hotel, just as soon as Miller's family gets out of there'?" shouted Mr. Glick, making sure he had heard correctly above all the noise.

"Yes, that's what I said. I'm a busy man. Is there anything else you want?"

"No, that is enough. Thank you very much."

Mr. Glick shouted in the direction of Liba and the boys, "I think now is a good time to leave." He began to run away from Mr. Olive and the pen; the children hurried behind him. Everyone jumped into the wagon and they were soon on their way back to the hotel, with "*WHO ... WHOO ... WHOOO*" still booming in their ears.

Chapter Nineteen

"Doesn't the color of the sandstone remind you of cheese blintzes?" Mrs. Glick asked Liba and the boys as they stood outside one of the feather palaces.

"Yes, the color is very similar," agreed Hershel. "And the color of the roof is just like the color of the cherry jam our mama used to make back in Kelm," he added.

"You know, I never thought of that before. It does look like cherry jam," said Mrs. Glick. She turned to Liba and asked, "It's very impressive, isn't it?"

"Yes, it is very pretty," Liba replied, distracted.

Earlier that morning, Mrs. Glick had offered to take Liba and her brothers to see a feather palace. The boys had immediately agreed; they had wanted to visit one ever since Mrs. Glick had first mentioned it weeks ago. Liba was not that interested; she had something else to do today that she felt was

very important. Chaim had eventually managed to convince her to come, telling Liba that it wouldn't be as much fun without her.

"What's that over there?" asked Peretz, pointing to a small tower sticking out from the side of the house.

"It's called a turret," Mrs. Glick explained.

"What does it do?" asked Peretz.

"Do? It doesn't do anything. It is just there for decoration."

"And what's that sitting high on top of the roof, on a little stand?" asked Chaim, pointing high in the sky.

"It's a chicken, fashioned from metal."

"A metal chicken? Why would anyone want a metal chicken?"

"To lay metal eggs, of course," explained Peretz, with a little smile.

"Really, Mrs. Glick? Does it really lay metal eggs?" asked Chaim.

"No, Peretz is just teasing you. It is there simply for decoration, just like everything else."

Mrs. Glick told them a number of interesting facts: Two gardeners were employed full time to keep the lawn green and the garden beautiful;

"It's a chicken, fashioned from metal,"
says Mrs. Glick.

the huge porch had taken three months to build; and the thick wooden shutters on either side of the bay windows had been made from a special type of wood called teak, imported all the way from India. The boys peppered Mrs. Glick with all sorts of questions. How many bedrooms were inside? How many staircases? How did they manage to wash the windows at the very top? And if the people who lived here had children, were these children ever allowed to play inside, in such a fancy house?

Liba wasn't really listening to the conversation. She was thinking about the night her family had first arrived in Oudtshoorn. Back in Kelm, she had spent hours imagining how beautiful Uncle Binam's hotel was, and how wonderful it would be to live there. Both she and Bayla were certain that the photograph on Uncle Binam's postcard was of the hotel; how shocked Liba had been when she arrived and realized her mistake. The photograph had nothing to do with Miller's Hotel; rather, it was of something called a feather palace.

How things had changed! Liba now loved Miller's Hotel; it was her home. She no longer had any desire to live in a feather palace. She was very happy with what she had and didn't ever want to move, to live anywhere else in Oudtshoorn. Thankfully, it didn't look as if she would have to.

As soon as Mr. Glick had returned from Olive's Ostrich Farm, he had told Itzig and Sorel about everything that Mr. Olive had said. He and Itzig had immediately gone to speak with Mr. Bartlett, the lawyer. This time, instead of taking one dozen potato kugels with them, they took the newspaper article that described Mr. Minty's recent arrest. Mr. Bartlett immediately made a few phone calls, and within two days, a letter from the Ministry of Public Works, marked "Special Delivery," was delivered to the hotel. Addressed to Mr. Itzig Miller, it stated that his property, located at 15 Albert Street, Oudtshoorn, had been built completely to code, and that it conformed to all standards and regulations. It had concluded with a sentence that read, "We regret any confusion and/or misunderstanding that may have been caused by one of our former employees."

Over the next few days, after Mr. Olive was

taken away for questioning by the local police, the story began to unfold. Mr. Olive had been desperate to build his emporium on the site of Miller's Hotel; it was the perfect location — just down the street from the Royal Crown. He hoped that guests staying at the luxurious hotel would be his regular customers, and that soon he would become very wealthy. When Liba heard this, she had found it very hard to understand. Wasn't Mr. Olive a successful ostrich farmer and feather dealer? Didn't he already have a lot of money? Yes, he did, her tatty had replied, but he obviously wasn't satisfied with what he had; he wanted more.

After a few more minutes spent admiring the feather palace, Mrs. Glick said it was time to go back to the hotel. She had left a chocolate cake cooling on a rack in the kitchen and she wanted to ice it before lunch. Liba was happy to return, but the boys were disappointed. They had wanted to see another feather palace. Mrs. Glick told them that if they left now, they would have time to help her ice the cake — if, of course, they first thoroughly washed their hands. The offer interested all of them, and they immediately agreed that they could visit another feather palace a different day.

As soon as they entered the hotel, the boys dashed into the kitchen, and Liba headed for her room. She noticed with satisfaction that everything she had prepared earlier was exactly as she had left it on her small desk: the quill, the pot of ink, the sheet of paper and the envelope. With a happy feeling inside, she smoothed out her dress, sat down and began to write:

Dear Bayla,

Thank you so much for your letter. I was happy to get it! I am sorry it has taken me so long to reply, but I have been very, very busy. I have so much to tell you and I am not sure where to begin, so I'll begin by telling you about something that I just learned — but not at school. (My mama told me that it is still summer vacation here and I don't have to start school for a few more weeks.)

Remember that Shabbos afternoon last summer when we were studying *Pirkei Avos* and you said that you were happy with what you have, but you had always thought you would be happier if you had more? You even mentioned it as a P.S. in your letter to me. Well, after everything that has happened here these past few weeks in Oudtshoorn, I finally appreciate the meaning of *"Eizehu ashir? Hasamei'ach b'chelko."*

Let me tell you how it all started ....

Glossary

Babka (Polish) — twisted yeast cake usually made in a high loaf pan

Blatt Gemara (Yidd.) — page of Talmud

Brachah (Heb.) — blessing

Bruchim haba'im (Heb.) — welcome

Chas v'shalom (Heb.) — Heaven forbid

Cheder (Yidd.) — primary school for Jewish studies

Chessed (Heb.) — kindness

Danke (Yidd.) — thanks

Daven (Yidd.) — pray

Fenster (Yidd.) — window

Hashem (Heb.) — the Almighty

Havdalah (Heb.) — blessing recited on Saturday night that separates between the Sabbath and the rest of the week

Kipferl (Yidd.) — crescent-shaped cookies made with almonds

Kugel (Yidd.) — baked pudding, usually made from noodles or potatoes

Lokshen (Yidd.) — noodles

Lulavim (Heb.) — palm branches, used to celebrate the holiday of Sukkos

Maariv (Heb.) — evening prayers

Minchah (Heb.) — afternoon prayers

Minyanim (Heb.) — quorums of ten adult Jewish men needed for public prayer

Mohn (Yidd.) — poppy-seed

Motzei Shabbos (Heb.) — Saturday night after nightfall

Pesach (Heb.)— the holiday of Passover

Pirkei Avos (Heb.) — Ethics of the Fathers

Purim (Heb.)— holiday that commemorates the Jewish people being saved from the plans of the wicked Haman to destroy them, during the time of the Persian empire

Samovar (Russ.)— a decorated tea urn used in Russia

Sefer Torah (Heb.) — Torah scroll

Shalom aleichem (Heb.) — peace be upon you; traditional Jewish greeting

Shtiebel (Yidd.) — a small, informal synagogue

Shul (Yidd.) — synagogue

Smous, smouse (Afrikaans) — peddler(s)

Tamar (Heb.) — palm tree

Teiglach (Yidd.) — small, knotted pastries boiled in a honeyed syrup

Zichrono livracha (Heb.) — of blessed memory

Mrs. Glick's Mushroom-Barley Soup

(It works wonders.)

Ingredients:

1 tsp. oil
2 large onions, peeled and chopped
3 stalks celery, trimmed and chopped
3 tbsp. water
3 cloves garlic, minced
8 cups hot water
3 potatoes, peeled and chopped
3 carrots, peeled and chopped
2 cups mushrooms, trimmed and sliced
½ cup pearl barley, rinsed and drained
freshly ground pepper, salt to taste
(You may add 2 tbsp. minced parsley and/or ¼ cup dill sprigs to taste. You may also add 1 tsp. dried basil, and/or ½ tsp. dried thyme to taste.)

Directions:

Heat oil on medium heat in large soup pot. Add onions and celery. Sauté for 5 to 7 minutes, until golden.
Add a little water once onions start to brown, to prevent sticking.
Stir in garlic and sauté 2 to 3 minutes longer.
Add remaining ingredients except seasonings.
Bring to a boil. Reduce heat, cover and simmer for approximately 1 hour. Stir occasionally, until barley is tender. If soup is too thick, add additional water.
Season to taste.

Yield: 10 servings. Reheats and/or freezes well.